Advance Praise for *Garden for the Blind*

"In *Garden for the Blind*, Kelly Fordon has situated her stories such that they dazzle with the immediacy of deeply felt life even as together they awe with the epic sweep of a life lived. Each story finds its peculiar curiosity in the midst of blight and rends the reader's heartstrings with the love the character has for it. An unforgettable first collection."
—Daniel Mueller, author of *Nights I Dreamed of Hubert Humphrey* and *How Animals Mate*

"*Garden for the Blind* is one of the most intricately and beautifully constructed works of fiction I've read. It is full of characters and interiors that are so fully realized they are impossible to think of strictly on the page. This is both an intense and page-turning adventure over which you will linger with awe at the precision and grace of its sentences and images. Kelly Fordon is a writer to admire, and to keep an eye on, and this work is one I'm never going to forget."
—Laura Kasischke, author of *Mind of Water* and *Eden Springs* (Wayne State University Press, 2010)

"Fordon's beautifully rendered stories chart the terri͡ created by polarities in race, gender, and social class ͡ oung woman in particular to transcend t͡ t it means to be a moral human b͡
—Eileen Pollack, former ͡ arts program at Universit͡ author of *Breaking ͡ ng*

"Kelly Fordon's profound and deeply moving stories ask how you deal with the unbearable truths of your life: the missteps and missed chances. Fordon's characters have to navigate a world of cynical politics and easy drugs. They long for their own identity but are lost in the demands the world makes of them. They want a set of rules in which to live their lives of easy comfort and killing neighborhoods. These stories are at once unsentimental and tender and you won't forget them."

—Gloria Whelan, National Book Award winner and
author of *Living Together* (Wayne State University Press, 2013),
which received the 2014 IPPY Silver Medal Award

"A strikingly atmospheric and psychologically acute collection of linked stories about the long-lasting reverberations of a childhood accident."

—Jenny Offill, author of *Dept. of Speculation*

"Each of Kelly Fordon's stories is perceptive, memorable, and moving—but taken together, they compose something far more significant: a tragicomic elegy for American youth as we knew it in the late twentieth century. I loved this book, and I will be haunted by its recurring characters for some time to come."

—Julia Glass, author of *And the Dark Sacred Night*
and National Book Award–winning *Three Junes*

"*Garden for the Blind* is a unique and constantly engaging collection of linked stories in which we are richly rewarded by a greater scope and a larger sense of the generations in play in this entertaining array of fictions. This book is a true joy to read, and a wonderful debut."

—Fred Leebron, professor of English at Gettysburg College
and author of *In the Middle of All This*

garden

for the

blind

MADE IN MICHIGAN WRITERS SERIES

*A complete listing of the books in this series can
be found online at wsupress.wayne.edu*

garden
for the
blind

stories by
kelly fordon

Wayne State University Press

Detroit

19 18 17 16 15   5 4 3 2 1

∞

Library of Congress Control Number: 2014956954

ISBN: 978-0-8143-4104-9 (paperback)
ISBN: 978-0-8143-4105-6 (ebook)

Publication of this book was made possible by a generous
gift from The Meijer Foundation. Additional support provided
by Michigan Council for Arts and Cultural Affairs and
National Endowment for the Arts.

Designed and typeset by Bryce Schimanski
Composed in Adobe Caslon Pro

There is only one time

when it is essential to awaken.

That time is now.

Buddha

contents

the

great gatsby

party

1974

W hen the Secret Service agents climbed up into the large oak trees lining the perimeter of the yard, Alice Townley thought they looked like giant tarsiers. She had seen tarsiers in her picture book about wild animals called *Do You Know What's Out There?* According to the book, tarsiers looked like teddy bears, but they were mean and would eat you if you startled them. The fact that there were tarsiers in the trees meant there was a special guest coming to the party, one who needed protection. It had not occurred to Alice, five, and her sister, Queenie, seven, to ask why.

All day their mother had been threatening to rename the party "The Great Fish Fly Party" rather than "The Great Gatsby Party." Even though everyone knew the annual hatch might be a problem in late June, it was the only time the vice president could make it to Michigan. Now, their imposing redbrick colonial was blanketed from top to bottom with smelly, creepy-looking insects, even though Pete, the gardener, had hosed it down three times since morning.

As the guests arrived, Alice and Queenie watched from their attic fort, a crawlspace they entered through a small door cut into the sloped wall off the attic playroom. Men in striped suits and straw hats and ladies in fringed dresses with wide bands on their hair spilled out of the French doors into the backyard, talking and drinking and picking fish flies off their clothes by the wings.

The crawlspace continued clear around to the front of the house, so after a little while, Queenie and Alice headed over to the other side for a view of the front yard. A group of a dozen or more people with matted hair and torn clothing had gathered on a grassy slope across the street from their house. Queenie told Alice the dirty people were angry about something their father was doing at his automobile company, but she wasn't sure what. Earlier in the day when the angry people first showed up, Alice's mother had called them "hippies" and said something about drugs. Their father shook his head and said they were probably just young and confused. Alice thought they looked dirty. Some of their signs showed a man on a throne and some had drawings of guns billowing smoke and some included words in bright-red or black capital letters that Queenie said were what Sister Angela called "profanity."

The party had been going on for an hour when Queenie announced that she was *starving to death*. Normally their mother didn't allow treats because she was afraid of Alice and especially Queenie, the beauty, "getting pudgy," but since the caterers (who Queenie and Alice called penguins because of their black-and-white uniforms) had taken over the kitchen and their nanny, Mrs. Miller, was helping usher in the guests, the coast was clear. Stealing desserts from catering trays was an art their brother Ray had taught them before he'd left for boarding school and summer camp, before he'd started lifting cigarettes and liquor instead of food.

Queenie ordered Alice to go to the kitchen and bring back something good.

"I always have to do it," Alice said. "Why don't you go?"

"You heard me," Queenie said in a menacing voice. She sat up straight to remind Alice who was bigger.

When Ray was home, Queenie and Alice stuck together, but now that Ray was away at camp, Queenie had turned into the Wicked Witch of the West. She was even worse than Ray because she sometimes locked Alice in the crawlspace when she was mad. One time she'd kept Alice prisoner for four hours, so long that Alice threw up into one of her mother's Louis Vuitton suitcases. Ever since then Alice made sure she was the closest one to the door.

"Jerk face," Alice muttered. *A real pain in my backside.* Their mother's expression. Just thinking it made her feel better.

"Hurry," Queenie said, handing her a large Hudson's shopping bag from the pile in the corner of the crawlspace.

Alice almost stuck out her tongue, but then she realized that Queenie had told her to hurry because she was scared. Queenie hated being left alone in the fort.

Serves you right, Alice thought.

Alice started down the servants' staircase that led right into the kitchen, but she found the door at the bottom of the staircase bolted shut. Probably Mrs. Miller didn't want any of the penguins wandering up to her room. She turned and ran back up the stairs and down the long narrow hallway to the front staircase.

In the bar there was a long oak bar top, a card table, and a floor-to-ceiling mirror. In front of the mirror a row of fake peace lilies were planted in pots lined with white pebbles. Her father was standing behind the bar along with the waiter giving out drinks. No one in the bar was paying any attention to her, so Alice stopped in front of the mirror and growled softly, pretending to be a tiger. "Tigers" was Queenie and Alice's favorite game, far better than *The Brady Bunch* game or Barbies, because they got to hide in the woods and creep around in the yard. Tigers were dangerous; they snuck up on you and *wham!* Alice couldn't believe that an enormous saber-toothed tiger could surprise anybody, but Queenie had insisted no one sees a tiger coming "until it's too late."

In the kitchen, the penguins pitter-pattered in and out carrying large trays. Alice hid underneath the sunflower-yellow Formica table, and when the penguins rotated out of the room she lifted a tray of cream puffs and upended them into her paper bag.

On the way back to the fort, she ran into a man's large knee as she was hurrying through the living room. He backed away from her, one hand over his heart.

"It's a child!" he exclaimed. A skinny lady in an emerald-green gown with hair as black and shiny-looking as a crow's grabbed hold of Alice. For a brief moment, the man and lady leaned in and looked at her. Their breath smelled like smoke and medicine.

"Who is she?" the woman said.

"Gerard and Michelle's daughter."

"They have children?"

"Two, maybe three. I think one's at camp."

"I never know what's coming next!"

The man shook his head. He jangled his limbs as if he might collapse. Several people laughed at the idea that a tiny girl had thrown him off-balance, but when he raised his drink to his lips, his hand was shaking.

"They're here!" Alice's mother yelled from the foyer, and the small crowd examining Alice dissolved and congealed again in a semicircle around the front door.

Alice inched along the wall from the living room to the grand staircase and crawled up a few steps so that she could see the front door over the heads of the partygoers. Her mother opened the door a smidge and peeked out.

"What's the password?" she said, looking back to wink at the people behind her. Everyone had been instructed to give a password on entering the party. Alice knew this because originally Queenie was the one who was supposed to stand at the door and ask each arrival for the password. Of course their mother had asked Queenie, because Queenie was her pet, the one that her mother called "Miss America." Whenever her mother hosted her tennis team or her bridge club, she walked Queenie around like a show pony. But Alice had also heard her mother say that Queenie was going to be "trouble" and Alice thought this was right. Queenie was giving her trouble every single day.

On the morning of The Great Gatsby Party, Queenie had said, no, she wouldn't wear the Nixon mask. "It smells!" she'd yelled, before flinging it on the ground and running off.

"Imogene Townley, get back here!" their mother had yelled. "I'm not asking you, I'm telling you!"

As Queenie fled up the stairs, their mother turned to Alice, and for a moment Alice thought she might be chosen as Queenie's replacement.

"Go upstairs and play," her mother said, with a dismissive wave. "I can't get anything done with you underfoot."

Now her mother picked up the mask and was putting it on herself.

"What's the password, dear?" Alice heard the man on the other side of the front door ask.

"Gordon, dear," a woman's voice answered.

"Gordon," the man repeated.

"Then I'll Liddy you right in!" her mother said, opening the door and flinging her arms out in welcome. The Nixon mask looked like Silly Putty and her mother had to hold it in place because it kept slipping down. Everyone clapped and laughed. The man in the doorway was tall. His face reminded Alice of vanilla pudding swirled with a spoon. The woman was holding a long cigarette holder out to one side. The glowing tip grazed the wall near the gilt mirror, but just as Alice was starting to worry about a fire, the woman stepped into the room.

"You are too much, Michelle!" The woman leaned into Alice's mother and waited for her to remove the mask so she could give her a peck on the cheek.

"I couldn't resist," her mother said. "Don't you look beautiful, Betty!" Then she turned back to the crowd behind them to announce their arrival.

"Vice President and Betty Ford!"

Everyone whooped and clapped and Alice watched the man and his wife parade into the room. She couldn't understand why her mother, whose voice had sounded wobbly, had called the woman beautiful—she was old and skinny and she walked sideways like Queenie's hermit crab.

Alice headed back up to the fort holding her goodies in the paper bag. Queenie had opened the window and was leaning out. Animal-like noises rose up from the street. Alice joined her to look at the people booing and shaking their fists at her house. When Queenie saw the bag, she grabbed it to rummage through.

"Cream puffs!" she squealed, popping one in her mouth.

That night Queenie had brought three books up to the crawl-space: *The Little Princess, The Secret Garden,* and *The Land of Oz.*

When Mrs. Miller wasn't busy drinking tea with Mrs. Cooper, the housekeeper, she sometimes muttered through a page or two, and they had gathered the gist of each story, the pictures filling in where Mrs. Miller left off. Alice's favorite was *The Little Princess* because of the secret gifts Sara receives from Ram Dass. Alice always dreamt about having her own Ram Dass, someone to save her from Mrs. Miller. This was Mrs. Miller's sixth child-rearing position in thirty-four years, she told anyone who would listen, and it would definitely be her last. Every time their parents left the house Mrs. Miller sat down to watch *Lawrence Welk* or *Coronation Street* with Mrs. Cooper and yelled at Alice and Queenie if they bothered her with nightmares or requests for food.

"Serves you right," she'd reply, if Queenie or Alice said they were hungry. "I made you a good dinner and you didn't touch it." By a good dinner, she meant liver and onions or Irish stew—food that made Alice gag.

Alice took a seat opposite Queenie and opened *The Land of Oz*. Queenie handed her the cream puffs. The people across the street started singing.

"Look!" Queenie said, showing the cream between her teeth. Alice screwed her face up. They went back to reading until the singing grew louder.

"It sounds like they're shouting more than singing," Alice said, pointing to the window.

Queenie stood back up. Alice followed. They leaned out the window again. The sun looked like an orange lollipop between the pine trees. The people sang a song about hard times and repeated the words "hard times" over and over. They swayed back and forth with their arms linked.

"Let's go outside," Queenie said.

"We're not allowed," Alice said, stepping back from the window.

"Nobody will see us," Queenie said, grabbing Alice's hand.

"I don't feel like it." Alice wrenched her hand away, but Queenie reached out and grabbed her arm, pinching the soft skin on her upper arm until she squealed.

"Stop it!"

"Come on then, or I'm telling Mom you stole all this food."

Alice wanted to call Queenie a jerk or a fatso, but Queenie was too scary. One time, Alice had called her a jerk and Queenie had pulled her pants down and spanked her with a hair brush.

Queenie started down the stairs and Alice followed, rubbing her arm. When they reached the French doors that opened onto the back yard, they had to weave their way through the crowd of partygoers. Queenie held fast to Alice's hand, dragging her along. Alice felt the eyes of the tarsiers on them as Queenie led her around the house to the front gate.

Across the street, the people were sitting along the curb. Some had their arms around each other as they sang. Others had candles, which they were holding up, and still others held lighters.

"They look sick," Alice said.

"I think they're hungry," Queenie said. "Get the cream puffs."

Alice made a face.

"Sister Angela says we should share," Queenie said.

Alice didn't move.

"Go!" Queenie said.

When Alice returned with the bag, they stood on the front lawn directly across from the people. There were so many. More than Alice had originally thought.

"They look mad," Alice whispered. "I want to go back."

Queenie grabbed Alice's hand and squeezed it.

"Ow!" Alice yelled.

"Serves you right," Queenie said. She was just about to cross the street when one of the tarsiers clamped a hand down on her shoulder.

"Where are you going?" he said. He was a young man with black hair. He reminded Alice of Father Michael, the new pastor, especially around the mouth, which wrinkled like a peach pit when he frowned.

"To give these out," Queenie said.

"Unhand them," one of the people across the street shouted. "Pig!"

"My mom said we should give them something to eat," Queenie said to the tarsier.

"She did?"

"Yes," Queenie said, holding up the bag. The tarsier reached in and grabbed a cream puff.

"Just be quick," he said, before jamming a whole thumbprint cookie into his mouth and handing back the bag. "I'm watching you."

Alice and Queenie crossed the street, the fish flies crackling under their sneakers. The smell of fish made Alice felt sick. The first person in the line was a girl with red hair. She looked like Renee, a college girl who sometimes babysat when Mrs. Miller was on vacation, and who spent all of her time in the kitchen on the phone laughing and twirling the cord into jumbled bunches around her finger.

Queenie held the bag up to her and the girl shut her eyes before reaching in. She pulled out a cream puff and kept her eyes squeezed tight as she popped it in her mouth.

"Groovy," she said drawing the last vowel out, mouth open and full of white goo. She didn't seem embarrassed. Alice glanced at the house to make sure her mother wasn't watching.

A girl with blue and gold beads in her hair said Queenie was cute and a boy with shaggy jean shorts mussed up Queenie's hair. Queenie smiled. She let go of Alice's hand and held the bag out to each person. Everyone waited for Queenie to come to them. She made her way down the line saying she only had enough for one each.

A boy with a yellow bandanna tied around his forehead yelled, "One for all and all for one!" and they all laughed.

Queenie was near the end of the row when the front door opened. All around Alice, people rose to their feet. The vice president and his wife appeared, followed by Alice and Queenie's parents. The wife was still holding her long cigarette holder. From across the street, Alice's house looked like a house in a picture book. The floodlights ran up the pillars like spikes.

The crowd booed and hissed, but the vice president and his wife never looked up. They studied the ground, his hand on her elbow as they continued down the front steps to a waiting limousine.

A man in a black cap emerged from the driver's side of the car and helped them both in. The crowd surged forward. Alice and Queenie were caught in the middle. Alice could feel hot, smelly bodies pressing in on her. She grabbed hold of Queenie's hand but then lost it when someone pushed between them.

"Alice!" Queenie yelled. "Alice!"

Alice froze and the people rushed past her.

The windows on the limousine were dark and no one could see inside but the crowd banged on the car anyway. The man with the yellow bandanna gave a rebel yell and leapt up onto the hood. He rose, standing on top of the car, and beat his chest; then he leaned in and peered through the blackened glass.

"Get lost!" he yelled.

"Go back to Grand Rapids where you belong!" someone else cried.

The tarsiers who were on the ground came running and others descended from the trees. They grabbed the man's hands, wrestling him off the car. Several other people leapt up onto the hood. They had to be pulled off one by one.

Queenie took Alice's hand, and they retreated to the grassy slope across the street from the house. The crowd rocked the car back and forth. Alice wondered whether it might tip over.

"We have to get back to the fort," Queenie said.

"No, Queenie!" Alice dropped down on the grass and crossed her legs, hiding her face in her hands.

"Come on. We'll pretend we're tigers."

"I'm scared," Alice said.

"You're stupid," Queenie said, getting down on her hands and knees. After a second, Alice did too.

Queenie growled and Alice growled back. Across the street some of the people, including the redheaded girl, continued to rock the car, while others fended off the tarsiers.

"Go on," Queenie said.

"I don't want to go first," Alice said.

"I said go!" Queenie said.

Chicken! Alice thought.

Alice crawled toward the house with Queenie behind. They were tigers. They were stealthy and powerful and sleek. The street was clear. Alice looked both ways. She inched out onto the gravel, which hurt her knees. Fish flies squished between her fingers.

Once they got back upstairs she would tell Queenie that she was going to bed. She wouldn't listen to her anymore. She'd lock herself in her room with her books and pretend that Queenie didn't exist. If Queenie didn't stop, she would tell Ray when he got home and maybe Ray would beat Queenie up or pull the heads off all of her Barbies or put real spiders in her bed. Real spiders were the best idea. She could just see Queenie's face.

Alice reached the other side of the road and sat down on the grass next to the driveway. Queenie wasn't far behind. The man in the yellow bandanna was standing on the edge of the driveway a few feet away, yelling at a tarsier. Other protesters were being pushed out of the driveway and into the yard, where a line of the tarsiers held them back. A large tarsier with black curly hair clapped a hand on the hood of the limousine.

"Move, move!" he yelled.

The car screeched as it turned out onto the street. Queenie was almost to the curb. She raised a hand against the glare of the headlights. Alice squeezed her eyes and clapped her hands over her ears. She heard the thud anyway.

Serves her right, Alice thought.

Then, there was no sound at all. Not when her mother ran down the driveway and flung herself on Queenie and then had to be pulled off by several of the hippies. Not when Dr. Mitchell, her father's best friend, pushed through the crowd to put his ear to Queenie's chest. And not even later, when the ambulance driver and his assistant placed Queenie gently on the gurney. Not when Mrs. Miller scooped Alice up and carried her into the house past her father, who was sitting on the front step with his face in his hands. No sound for a long time afterward. Just people moving their mouths, hurrying this way and that.

use everything

in your

arsenal

੨ֆ

1980

All of the neighborhood kids were playing "shark attack" when we heard a whooping cowboy call.

"Yah! Yah! Yah!"

We couldn't see who was yelling, but we heard the smack of fast feet on the sidewalk. In our imaginary lands, we were always under attack. It was 1980, that time before Atari transfixed kids in basements across the nation and parents had not yet started fighting back with summer-long wilderness camps. In those pre-video-game days, every kid we knew spent the summers roaming aimlessly. My brother Peter was nine and I was eleven. We lived in a small suburb just outside of Indianapolis where there was nothing to do but make up alternate lives far more exciting than the ones we were living.

Peter yelled, "Up! Up! *Up!*"

We clamored to the top of the jungle gym expecting Al Capone or an insane garbage man to appear. Instead, a little boy Peter's size rounded the corner of the house. A shock of white hair sprang up fountain-like on the top of his head. A crossbow was slung across his back. He was skinny, dressed in saggy army fatigues and a tight black T-shirt. His thin white arms looked as flimsy as the miniblinds Mother was peeking out of behind him. He turned round and round on the lawn with a knife in hand, poised as if he were in the jungle doing recon. In his other hand, he had an entire ammunition dump, which he let clatter to the ground once he was in position.

Everything turned on that moment. Or so it seemed later.

"Cool," Peter said, climbing down. "Where'd you get all those guns?"

"My dad," the kid yelled. It sounded like he had a mouthful of gumballs. Later we learned it was a Canadian accent. He had lived for a time in Toronto. His name, he said, was Michael Phineas Gallagher.

"What kind of a name is Phineas?" Peter yelled. He walked over and picked up a .38-special cap revolver.

"Some old dead somebody I was named after. Everybody calls me Mikey," he said. "My uncle Charlie says Phineas is a faggot's name."

There were a lot of born-again Christians on the block and four of them—George Patterson, Drew Mayer, Eric Brewer, and Hayden Allen—were in the yard that day. All of the born agains attended Bible Community Church and all of their parents were strongly opposed to violence. Every time a fight broke out in a born again's backyard, a parent would emerge and suggest we "take it to the peace table."

Kids made weapons out of sticks and broken bats and old rusted pipes. They whittled knives out of broken branches. They fashioned grenades out of pinecones. But real toy weapons—store-bought weapons, weapons that looked like weapons? That was new and tantalizingly wicked.

It wasn't long before everyone else climbed down from the jungle gym to examine Mikey's booty. He distributed every piece in his arsenal. I took an M-80; a pacifist in theory, I was no extremist. We organized into enemy lines and lit off down the street, Mikey in the lead.

That day our nanny, Jacinta, had to scour the neighborhood before she finally found us in Mikey's yard in the midst of a battle for control of the new lime-green swing set. "I'm a look for you everywheres," she said. "You know what time you go home, Johnny!" She pointed to the sky. It was dark.

I left with her but it took several more shouts to rouse Peter out and she was so mad we could barely keep up as she barreled down the street ahead of us.

"Isn't he the best, Johnny?" Peter said.

"Yeah," I said.

"See you guys tomorrow," Mikey called after us. "Bright and early. I'll sound the battle cry."

"My dinner it all burnt now!" Jacinta fumed as we made our way home. "But you better make like it taste better than birthday cake."

At first, my father thought Mother's incoherent babbling was a by-product of life on a zealot-infested street. In the end, he would have given anything for that to be the case. Over the past three years, she'd been hospitalized more often than not. Our housekeepers, Jacinta and Maria, were hired when she first started talking in tongues. Jacinta did all of the cooking and Maria cleaned. About once a month, they received letters and pictures from home. One time Jacinta set a picture down on the counter of a small girl in a white eyelet dress standing in front of a tiny, tin-roofed shack. She looked puzzled, as if she was wondering, "Where did my mommy go?"

Peter and I slept in a bunk bed in my bedroom. We kept all of our toys in Peter's bedroom. Downstairs Jacinta cooked. Maria slipped in and out of our rooms as wordless and wary as a cat. Mother remained secluded in her bedroom. Her strange behavior mortified me. Whenever Jacinta went in to check on her, I pictured Jesus venturing into Lazarus's tomb. Other people's mothers moved around in the daylight. When I had friends over, I always pretended that her ailments were temporary—flu, I said, a stomach bug, a headache. Not Peter. When his pals came over he'd point to her room and shrug, "My mother sleeps all day." Later, he was even less circumspect. The first time we brought Mikey up to the playroom, Peter yelled, "Wacko alert! Wacko alert!" when we passed her room. Mikey burst out laughing.

The day after Mikey appeared we made another intriguing discovery about him.

"My mother's a celebrity," he said. "Susan Gallagher, the new channel-seven news anchor. She's so good her boss says it won't be long before she's giving Baba Wawa a run for her money."

We told our father about our auspicious neighbor and he let us watch the news with him, which was a first. She was a beautiful woman with dark eyes, a big bright-red mouth, and hair almost as light as Mikey's. It fell to her shoulders in a sheet. Her hair, so static and straight, and her robotic recitation of the nightly news, reminded me of the mannequins in the Hudson's Department Store window display.

"She looks a little stiff," my father said, "but she's very professional." He seemed impressed by the arrival of a television personality on the street. All of his hard work at the bank had paid off—a beautiful house and a swanky neighbor to boot. After that, we struck up daylong baseball and dodgeball and soccer games on the vacant lot across the street from Mikey's house and rode our bikes past every chance we got, but we never caught a glimpse of her.

By July, Mikey had achieved legendary status on the block.

"He's got tons of comic books, he's got a huge candy stash in his room, he knows karate," Peter gushed. Every morning at seven, he headed out the door to wait for Mikey on the front lawn. I wasn't as geeked. All of Mikey's stories made my stomach churn. He told us about his mother's divorce, how she had caught his father with another woman. His mother had thrown the other woman into the bedroom wall. There was a hole where her head went through. Or so he claimed.

"Jeez!" I said to Peter, when Mikey was finished. "Can you imagine if that had happened to Mother? She probably wouldn't even have noticed the other woman! She probably would have just hopped into bed with them."

"Can't you just see it?" Peter laughed. "She'd plop down right on top of them. 'Oops!' she'd say. 'Excuse me!' And then she'd just wander back out into the hall."

According to Mikey, his mother's relatives were New York City snobs.

"My cousin Shelly went to the hospital to pick up her mum—that's my aunt Krissie—with this new baby Andrea. This nurse, this enormous Amazon with bright-red hair, had to wheel Aunt Krissie out to the car. Just as she was about to get up from the wheelchair, the fat bitch grabs Aunt Krissie's hair and yanks her head back."

He paused.

"She's yanking and yanking and she says, 'You are one uppity, uppity bitch! Good fucking luck to that poor baby!' Shelly said Aunt Krissie was just howling in pain. Uncle Rob had to pull that fat twat off her."

It didn't take much to worry me in those days and it wasn't long before Mikey began to frighten me. After he brought the *Playboy* up to the fort and tied a sparkler to our cat Whiskers's tail, I started to lose sleep. One day, on a whim, I asked Mother for advice. She was reading on the couch and something about the concentration with which she studied the book and the way she licked her finger to turn the pages reminded me of the old days when she could be counted on to make the transition from one sentence to the next. I sat down on the couch across from her and waited for her to look up. When she did, I said, "I'm beginning to think Mikey is a total creep. He uses bad words. He lies. I think he stole twenty dollars from my drawer." I didn't add that when I'd confronted Mikey about the money, he'd produced a pocket knife, which he waved in my face, hissing, "I don't need your fucking money, loser."

"Hmm?" She blinked several times; her eyes were as wide and black as Susie Patterson's Baby Tender Love doll. "What was his name? Finnegan? Faustus? Is that the new boy?"

"He's been here for three months," I said.

"Really?"

"Forget it," I said, standing up. On my way out the door, I passed Jacinta, who, it turned out, had heard me.

The following morning she caught Mikey as he was coming through the side door. "I know what you do to Johnny," she said.

I was at the top of the stairs listening. Peeking through the banisters, I could just make out the top half of the front door. Mikey tried to slide in past her. She grabbed his shirt and pulled him toward her.

"What I do to Johnny?" He grinned and cocked his head.

"No bad magazines. No bad words. If you steal, you no come."

"Yes, ma'am," he said, saluting.

It was the first time it occurred to me that if Mother wasn't available there might be other options.

After a long afternoon on the jungle gym, Jacinta would call us in for dinner. Peter leapt down and raced for the door. But every day I grew heavier and heavier, as if my shoes were filled with sand. If Mother made it to the dinner table those nights, I ignored her. I sat in my chair like a stone, not touching Jacinta's fried bananas and fish. If my father put the newspaper down and asked us about our day, I didn't answer. One day we heard someone whooping in the backyard and when Mother asked who it was, I told her it was Faustus.

"Really?" she said. She got up, went out to the backyard, and reappeared a minute later with Mikey in hand.

No one spoke much at the dinner table at my house. My father read the paper. Mother stared into space. Peter and I made faces at each other.

Mikey didn't know the rules.

"Chow time!" he shouted, tucking his napkin into the collar of his T-shirt. "You guys have no idea how hungry I am."

Mother turned to him and in the automated voice that was a by-product of the medication, said, "When was the last time you ate?"

"This morning, a Pop-Tart. I don't always go back for lunch, ya know, with Maureen, my babysitter, being the big bitch she is . . . excuse me, ma'am . . . being kind of mean, I don't like her."

Mother chewed on her lower lip and stared at him for a long time.

"I knew a boy like you once," she said. "His name was Pip. He also had great expectations."

Peter and I looked at each other. Mikey stared at Mother, his lips quivering as if he was battling a laugh.

"Oh?" he said, finally. "That's too bad."

"Yes," she said. "It is."

After that, we ate in silence for several minutes until Mikey said, "I noticed you sleep a lot. Are you sick?"

Mother put down her fork. "I'm glad you asked," she said.

My father looked up from the paper. "What's this?" he said.

"This little boy has just asked me what's wrong," Mother said. She reached out and patted Mikey softly on the head. "I love this white hair." When he flinched, she stood up abruptly and placed her right hand on her chest as if she were reciting the Pledge of Allegiance.

"It's funny that you think I'm sleeping. Sleeping is funny, or is funny sleeping? Funny to sleep when you're feeling funny. Feeling funny? Feeling sleepy? I'm not sleeping. Sometimes when you think I am sleeping, I am . . ." She stopped and looked over at my father, who was giving her the weary look one might give a child who has peed in his bed again.

"I don't know that it's any of your business, young man." My father turned his defeated gaze on Mikey. "It's not polite to ask people about their ailments."

"I'm not sleeping. I'm not sleeping." Mother rotated toward me. "I am . . ."

She was staring straight ahead now. Her eyes had glazed over. Peter shot me a look. He got up from the table and shuffled over to the sink. Jacinta took his plate.

"That's enough, Rosemary," my father said. "Maybe you should go upstairs."

Looking like a member of the marching band executing an elaborate roundabout, Mother turned on her heel. Mikey stared at her, wide-eyed, the sides of his mouth twitching.

"I'm not sleeping. I'm not sleeping," she repeated as she marched in place.

"Rosemary!" my father hissed. "Go up and rest."

We all watched her march out of the room.

I got up and handed my plate to Jacinta. Normally she would have chastised me for not eating, but she took it and dumped it in the sink without glancing up. Mikey followed me. Peter was already waiting for us.

Mikey started laughing the minute the side door closed behind us. "Man, I thought my mom was fucked up, but you two . . . you guys? Man!"

After Mikey tied the sparkler to Whiskers's tail, the other mothers clued in to his antics. Parental conferences took place via phone and later on the stoop in front of Mrs. Brewer's house. I heard about it from Peter, who kept up on the neighborhood gossip. Mrs. Brewer's husband Ed owned the Village Market and all of his kids went to The New School. She did not want Mikey bringing his weapons into her yard. Interestingly, Mrs. Allen thought it was all right as long as we kept them outside. I was surprised because she had never allowed her kids to watch *Gilligan's Island* or *Happy Days*. I began to wonder at these arbitrary parental restrictions.

A couple of times when I went to the grocery store with Jacinta, we ran into Mikey, who was wandering up and down the aisles by himself. He waved at us as if it were totally normal for an eleven-year-old to be cruising through town by himself. The sight of him terrified me. I knew what he was capable of. He might steal something while I was looking. If he did, would I snitch? If I didn't, how would I live with that? My other fear was that he would pilfer something and stuff it down my shirt. I would get caught. The police would drag me away, and Jacinta wouldn't be able to convince them I was framed.

"Who takes care of that kid?" Mrs. Patterson was leading George and me through the line at Friendly's Ice-Cream Parlor. Mikey was sitting in a booth by himself eating a strawberry ice-cream cone. George and I shrugged. Mikey was the only person who regularly emerged from his house. We all decided that his mother must be teleporting to work. She was so furtive that no one could say for sure what kind of car she drove. Luke and Tommy said it was a black LTD. Peter thought he'd seen a navy-blue Pinto parked in the driveway, but the general consensus was "she couldn't drive that crapper."

One day Mrs. Brewer knocked on Mikey's door. The woman who answered was disheveled and swollen. Her clay-colored hair hung down like strips of papier-mâché. She had no shoes on and her ankles were as round as telephone poles. She looked like she had just climbed out of bed.

"I'm so sorry to bother you," Mrs. Brewer said. Even we kids could tell she was trying not to look shocked. It was eleven in the morning. "I'm Luke's mom." She gestured behind her, where a whole troop of us were stationed at the end of the lawn. Peter waved.

"Mikey keeps asking Eric over, but I have a policy. I like to meet the parents or caretakers or whoever is in charge before he goes over to someone's house."

The woman stared at her wordlessly. Mrs. Brewer fumbled a little in the silence, before adding, "I mean, I also wanted to welcome Mikey's family to the neighborhood."

"I'm Maureen," the woman said. She gave a quick twitch of her mouth in lieu of a grin. Her teeth were brown and crooked. Around her neck, she wore a gold-toned necklace with the letters "MO" worked out in rhinestones. Her white T-shirt had what looked like spaghetti stains down the front. "Mrs. Gallagher ain't home."

"Oh," Mrs. Brewer said.

Maureen peered out at us.

"Well, clearly I'll have to come back!" Mrs. Brewer laughed. "Let's go." She motioned to us.

"OK," Maureen said. She shut the door.

༃

The following week, Mikey came running into our yard looking as if he was being chased by a rabid animal. He dropped his bow, glanced up at us as if he had no idea how he'd ended up at our house, and then threw up all over the lawn.

"Gross!" Peter yelled, banging on his ears like he did every time we watched a horror movie.

I followed Mikey into the house. He walked past Jacinta and into the bathroom, holding the sleeve of his shirt up to the right side of his head. Mother looked up from her book and studied the bathroom door.

She got up from the couch. "Go outside, John."

"I'm waiting for Mikey."

"I said, *go outside!*"

"Jeez, whatever," I muttered.

They didn't come out again. Mother locked the side door so none of us could get in. I would have worried about Mikey if Jacinta and Maria weren't home.

We headed up to Eric's house. When I came back a couple of hours later, the side door was open and Mother was back on the couch reading her book.

"What was that all about?" I said.

"Inclement weather." She didn't look up.

"What's that supposed to mean?"

"The return flight is always bumpy."

I'd been standing there looking bewildered for well over a minute before she finally glanced up again.

"Nothing you need to worry about," she said, waving her hand dismissively.

"He's *my* friend!" I shouted, but she didn't even flinch.

"What's wrong with Mikey?" I asked Jacinta later that night.

"Maureen was mean." She kept slicing cucumbers and tomatoes, periodically wiping her large-knuckled hands on her white apron. "But he's going to be OK. Praise Jesus."

"What did she do?"

"She hit him."

"Hit him? Like a spanking?" Jacinta had wacked me before.

"Upside the head with her fist. Knocked him out."

"Unconscious?"

Jacinta nodded. "That's why he threw up."

"Jeez."

"But they got rid of her, so he be safe now."

"Is she coming back?"

"No, no, of course not!" Jacinta's eyes opened wide, as if she was horrified at the thought.

After the new nanny arrived, a tiny Asian woman named Shell, Mikey's behavior got worse. He got caught stealing candy from the toy store. He pulled a girl's pants down on the playground. He told Peter to "Fuck off!" at recess. Peter told the principal.

"Do you think he hates me?" Peter said. He thought Mikey had been kicked out of school for saying bad words, but the truth was that Mikey had been expelled for chucking his pencil case at his teacher. She was writing on the blackboard so she'd never seen it coming. She'd turned around just in time to catch it between the eyes.

That summer, Mikey was sent to his grandmother's in Bay City, which we later learned was part of his normal routine. He spent every summer with his grandmother because of his mother's busy work schedule. His aunt Krissie showed up to drive him just as Jacinta was passing by the house on her way to the Village Market. Jacinta knew we'd be interested in Mikey's destination so she stopped to chat with his aunt. She met Susan Gallagher as well, and reported that she looked like a Jezebel with all that paint on her face. Jacinta said that Mikey waved to her when he got into the car. According to Jacinta, he seemed happy.

"Wherever he goes," she said, "it goes better there."

Right after Mikey left for his grandmother's, Peter got sick in Mrs. Patterson's car on the way to the zoo. Flustered, Mrs. Patterson dropped him off at home without calling first. Jacinta was at the grocery store and Maria had gone home for three weeks to visit her family. He found Mother on the floor in her bathroom. She had taken a whole bottle of her pills. Her pale-blue nightgown was wedged up around her hips and she was surrounded by postcards. They were scattered all over the green tiles. Somehow, he was able to drag her back to the bed before calling 911.

The ambulance came and carted her off for her third hospital stay in as many months. I found the postcards still scattered on the bathroom floor later that afternoon. There were at least twenty of them. Hand-drawn pictures on the front, child-like drawings of a beach, a mountain, a tree. They were all addressed to my mother and they all said some variation of the same thing:

"Hello from Buenos Aires!"

"Happy Birthday from Rome!"

"Happy New Year from Sao Paolo, where it's nice and sunny!"

We were playing baseball across the street from his house when Aunt Krissie brought Mikey back. Instead of heading inside the house, he opened up the trunk of the car and grabbed his artillery. As we watched him run toward us shouting gladiator-style, it was clear that staying with his grandmother hadn't helped him at all.

Jacinta sat us down the next day and said, "Don't you mess around with that boy. I know your mother thinks he's OK, but I can see right through him."

She was preaching to the choir as far as I was concerned, but Peter didn't hear a word she said. Mikey came over every day. I usually spent the afternoons holed up in my room. One afternoon as I was reading on my bed, enjoying the peace and quiet and the warmth of the sunlight coming in from the window above me, there was a knock on the door.

"Your brother here?" Mikey walked in without asking and came to a stop next to the bed, where he leaned down to peer at the cover of my book. "Tom Sawyer . . . isn't that a baby's book?"

"I think Jacinta took him to the dentist." I put the book down and scooched up so I was sitting against the headboard.

He'd grown over the summer. He was closing in on me height-wise and he already had sinewy muscles in his arms, which I knew portended no good. He thumbed through the other books on my bookshelf and ambled around peering at my desk and my bedside table. In those days, I was afraid that whatever had claimed Mother would take hold of me and I kept a Bible on my bedside table for protection against demons.

Mikey eyed it. Then he picked it up and the postcards poured out.

I leapt up, yanking the Bible out of his hands. When I did that, he bent down and scooped up the postcards before I could get to them.

"Give me those!" I yelled. He had turned away from me and was facing the bookcase, flipping through them. When he turned back around, he was smiling. "Those are my mother's," I said.

"And who sent them to her, eh? A lover? Another crazy daisy? Someone she met in the institution?"

"Shut up!"

He held them out to me and I grabbed them.

"Who sent them, Johnny? Don't you know?"

I stared at him.

"You know what would be great? It would be great not to see your sad-sack, boring, end-of-the-fucking-world face every day. Is that all you can do? Make that stupid fucking face? Why don't you stop moping around and get a life?"

"You're a jerk," I whispered.

The next day Officer Rich Hess called my father at work and my father went to pick Peter up in jail where he and Mikey had spent the afternoon sitting on stools in the police department's tiny kitchenette. They'd lifted Pop-Tarts and sparklers from Safeway. Because we lived in such a small town, the jail only boasted one cell. Peter was disappointed that a "real criminal" was already occupying it.

My father grounded Peter for a month, but as things turned out the punishment ended a week later, forgotten because of what finally happened to Mother.

I was in my room reading the following afternoon. Mikey's taunting was eating at me. I was a coward. I spent my whole life tiptoeing around, trying not to get in anyone's way, trying not to upset Mother, trying not to bother my father, trying to pretend that everything was normal. I was a dolt and I was sick of it. There was no reason I couldn't simply ask her about the postcards. At least that might spark a conversation. At least then I could ask her outright what was wrong with her and how long she thought we would all have to put up with it. Peter would have thought I was crazy attempting a conversation, but he was too young to remember the days before everything fell apart—the afternoons spent playing chess and eating cookie dough straight out of the bowl, the trips to the zoo and the science museum.

I found her in the den watching Shirley Temple.

"I hope you're feeling better," I said. She had been back from the hospital for two weeks since the postcard incident. I'd heard my father tell Jacinta and Maria that he was hopeful the doctors had finally gotten the dosage right.

"I love this one." She pointed at the TV. I stared at her sunken face. Despite the new medication, she was still chewing on her lips. They were swollen and bruised.

"How are you feeling?" I said.

She didn't answer. Shirley had her mesmerized. I took a seat on the loveseat next to her couch and placed the postcards in my lap. "I've already finished my summer workbook. I'm thinking about asking Jacinta whether we can bake some chocolate-chip cookies."

"You'll never be done," she said.

At first I wasn't sure she was talking to me. She was staring at the television while Shirley sang "Animal Crackers in My Soup."

"I'm sorry?"

"There will always be more."

Normally that comment would have sent me packing, but that afternoon I was determined. We watched TV for a couple of minutes before I was able to push out the words. "I was wondering about these postcards," I said, tapping them against my leg.

Her head turned slowly, as if a tiny man inside was cranking it. "What?" she said.

I held the stack out to her. She was looking toward me but not quite at me.

"An old friend," she said, turning back to Shirley.

"No," I said. "I don't think so."

"Give me those." She held out her hand.

I handed them to her.

"Please leave me alone," she said.

"You wrote them, didn't you?"

She didn't answer. She wouldn't look at me.

"Why?" I started shaking. I was suddenly so angry I could barely control myself.

Shirley kept singing,

> When I get hold of the big bad wolf
>
> I just push him under to drown
>
> Then I bite him in a million bits
>
> And I gobble him right down

Jacinta came in carrying a laundry basket.

"I'd really like to know," I hissed. "I'd really like to know what kind of wacko sends herself postcards."

My tone caught Mother's attention and she looked over at me. When she opened her mouth, nothing came out.

"How long are you going to be like this?" My throat was raw. The words were coming out, but it was as hard as pushing gumballs through a straw. "What the hell is wrong with you?" I shouted.

"Johnny!" Jacinta shouted, dropping the laundry basket. "Johnny, you need to stop bothering your mother."

"What is wrong?" I said. "What the hell is wrong with you!"

Mother started to cry. She grabbed one of the throw pillows and buried her face in it.

Jacinta took my arm and dragged me out of the room. When we were standing in the hallway, she struck me on the side of the head with the flat of her hand. "What the matter with you? Your mother sick. You think she like it like this? You think she want this? What were you thinking?"

I turned and walked back to my room. I felt bad for making her cry, but I also felt like I'd been carrying a carcass around and could finally set it down.

A week later, I slept right through the final sirens.

Several weeks later, when I was still refusing to leave my room, my father forced me into counseling. Dr. Shivant, a kind, grandmotherly woman, thought she could guide me back to shore. I never let on that I couldn't even see land. Twenty years later, I'm still adrift. I look to the outside world like a replica of my banker father. I myself am a successful banker. I know how to play the game. I keep on rowing my boat despite the anchor. I'm the only one who knows I will never make any progress at all.

That fall, Mikey's mother landed a job anchoring the nightly news in Detroit, a much larger market than ours in Indianapolis.

After they moved, Mrs. Gallagher turned up every now and then on *The Today Show* when we were sitting in the kitchen with Jacinta and Maria, eating our Captain Crunch. I remember thinking that it would be wonderful to have a mother who was famous, one you could show off to your friends, one who was alive and well, but then I remembered that the reality had been quite different from the fantasy. Mikey had lived on our block for two years and I'd only seen his mother twice.

These days my brother and I talk once or twice a year. When I visited him last year outside Bozeman, we reminisced about Mikey.

"Mikey's mother was hot, but she might as well have been living on another planet." Peter was sloppy drunk. He leaned back against the wall. We were in his tiny hunting cabin, the one he retreats to more and more often these days in order to avoid his wife Sydney and their mounting financial problems. The cabin has a fireplace but no running water. Peter had his eyes closed, and because we'd just lit the fire and the place was still freezing, his breath was mushrooming up like plumes from a volcano. On the floor, one of his three dogs whined in its sleep.

"The hot part probably didn't make up for that," I said. "I wonder what ever happened to him?"

"I heard he went to Alaska," Peter said, exhaling smoke.

"No way."

"Then I heard he was in jail."

"That sounds more like it." I held out my hand and he passed me the cigarettes.

"Then I heard he lives on his own private island in the Caribbean."

"Who'd you hear that from?" I lit my cigarette. It was almost too cold to hold it.

"George Patterson. He and some buddies were out here hunting last year."

"Hmm. I wonder which story is true? I'm betting jail. Remember Whiskers and the sparklers?"

Peter chuckled and tamped out his cigarette into his cup before handing the cup to me. Then he got up from the bed and threw the blanket around his shoulders. "I've got to pee," he said.

"I still can't understand why you don't have indoor plumbing." I set the cup back down on the chipped coffee table. "Wherever Mikey is, I'm sure he's fine."

"Yes," Peter said, opening the door. A snow gust blew into the room, covering the floor and the bed. He ducked his head into the blanket. A couple of the dogs started barking and ran out into the night ahead of him.

Before he closed the door, he looked back at me. "One thing about him, he was well armed."

lucky

❧

1985

Alice got caught on a Tuesday. Her parents were on vacation so the principal had to call Aunt Rita, who lived way out in Clarkston. Of course Aunt Rita, dependent on Alice's father's goodwill, said that yes, she was babysitting, and yes, she would make sure Alice spent her entire three-day suspension at home under close supervision. Aunt Rita told Principal Altman that the housekeeper, Miss Powers, would be there shortly to pick Alice up.

Principal Altman hung up the phone. "Alice," he said. "You don't want to ruin your life with this stuff. I know you don't. You started out so well here and now look at these grades." He tapped a sheet of paper on his desk. "You're failing three classes. Your parents are paying a lot of money for this education and you're squandering it."

"Yes, sir," Alice said. "I know it. I'm going to do better. They're already on my case about my grades. I've been grounded for the past two weeks."

"They must be very disappointed, and now what are they going to say about marijuana possession, Alice? Do you know how this will look on your record?"

"Is it going on my record?" asked Alice.

"That depends on you," Principal Altman said. He took off his glasses and pinched the bridge of his nose. "We might be able to negotiate. I know you're just getting back on your feet. We might reconsider if you're willing to tell me who sold it to you."

Alice sat back in her chair and looked up at the clock over Mr. Altman's desk. The second hand looked like it couldn't bear to move forward. She was never going to get in any trouble and they both knew it. She wondered why he was bothering with the charade. Her parents, if they'd ever cared about smoking pot, had long since ceased, but Fox Grove High School cared about her parents' generous donations, and they were not going to kick Alice out.

"Can I think that over, Mr. Altman?" Alice said. "I hate to snitch on anyone."

"You have one day, Alice." He held up the baggie and shook it, and then, as if he realized he'd given her no incentive to squeal, he added, "And one more thing—if you don't give me a name, I'm just going to assume the dealer is your friend Michael Gallagher. Just so you know."

Mr. Altman sent his secretary with Alice to get her books out of her locker and make sure she left the premises. Thankfully, the hallways were empty.

Home was only three blocks away, but it took Miss Powers twenty minutes to turn up in her beat-up Chevy. When Alice got in the car, Miss Powers tsked and shook her head.

"Girl like you with everything going for you," she said. "You're going to throw it all away."

"No, I'm not," Alice said.

"Yes, you are. And for what? For nothing. If I'd had half the chances you've had, believe me, I wouldn't be here with you."

"Nice," Alice said.

It was hard to imagine Miss Powers, with her black sensible shoes and her chin whiskers and her rat-like bun, had ever had many options. She'd replaced the previous babysitter, Mrs. Miller, after Alice's sister Queenie was broadsided by a car ten years before. Of course, that had been just as much her parents' fault as anyone's. What was a seven-year-old doing in the street? The answer was that no one had been watching either of the girls during the Great Gatsby Party, because Alice's mother had asked Mrs. Miller, the babysitter, to help waitress. Even though Alice's mother was ultimately to blame, Mrs. Miller lost her job, and instead of paying more attention to their remaining children after that, her parents paid less.

When Miss Powers first came onto the scene, Alice had asked her mother where she came from as Miss Powers's accent was so pronounced.

"She came over here from England by herself," her mother said. "I don't think she has any family."

It turned out, upon investigation, that none of that was true. Miss Powers was Irish and she had plenty of family. Her mother had died young and Miss Powers had to raise her siblings and comfort her depressed father while trying not to sit or step on any of the family's eight cats. The whole long drawn-out incarceration (her word) had turned her off family obligations of any sort. Now she wanted to plan her own twice-yearly vacations and enjoy a little peace and quiet, a footstool, a telly, and some tea every afternoon at four. She'd been very unhappy with Alice the year before during what she referred to as the "unpleasantness," but she hadn't left. Alice guessed this was because her parents had increased Miss Powers's salary to compensate for the extra vigilance required last May when Alice had returned from Hartwick Psychiatric no longer suicidal but still saddled with her DSM III diagnosis, "severely depressed without psychotic tendencies." Though all of her psychiatrists believed witnessing Queenie's fatal accident was the root of the problem, Alice did not agree. She tried to explain that her sister had not even been that nice, but they insisted that she was suffering from sibling guilt and post-traumatic stress, and at the time she didn't have energy to argue.

Miss Powers turned off onto Main Street. "You know what I mean," she said to Alice. "If you think you're getting back at someone or you think someone else is going to bear the brunt of your bad behavior, you are wrong, little lady. It's you who'll pay."

"Yeah, yeah, yeah," Alice said. "Can we hit Shields on the way home?"

At Shields Diner, Alice bought herself mac and cheese and Miss Powers a Reuben, because as she was headed in, Miss Powers had said, "If there wasn't plenty at home and I wasn't watching my pennies, I would buy myself a Reuben sandwich."

There was plenty to eat at home, but eating at home had grown tedious. Alice's parents had been on the yacht for close to a month and weren't expected back for five more days. They'd left Alice alone with the cleaning staff, which consisted of the gardener; the head housekeeper, Miss Powers; two supplementary cleaners, both from China, whom Alice couldn't tell apart and whom she called Long and Dong behind their backs because their goofy affability reminded her of the Chinese exchange student, Long Duk Dong, in the movie *Sixteen Candles*; and the chauffeur, Mr. Richardson. Mr. Richardson hardly did a thing, but he lived above the garage and was "always on call." Alice's father had repeatedly warned her not to drive under the influence as he paid Mr. Richardson to be available around the clock. But Alice hated seeing Mr. Richardson eyeballing her through the rearview mirror and hated the underarm smell of him and always chose to drive herself no matter how inebriated she was. The town was small enough and the speed limit slow enough that Alice figured she'd need to be completely catatonic to veer off the road, and so far she'd been right. The worst thing she'd ever done was hit a curb and the right side of a mailbox before correcting the wheel.

When they returned to the house with the Shields takeout, Miss Powers thanked her for the Reuben, put it on top of the laundry in the basket she'd left in the hall, and continued on into the dark recesses of the house. The good thing about Miss Powers was that she seemed to think that being in the same building as Alice constituted care. She never overly concerned herself with Alice's activities in the house even when there were large groups of people hanging out in Alice's room until all hours. The next day Miss Powers just came in and cleaned up all the cups and wrappers and overturned liquor bottles and went on to the next chore.

Alice sat down at her desk with her mac and cheese and looked out over the long driveway, out toward the street where she could just barely make out the cars going by on MacArthur Avenue. Once upon a time, the Townley Estate had been an all-girls Catholic school situated on Lake St. Clair, and the nuns had planted elm trees down the length of the driveway, creating a beautiful canopied path. When they first moved in, Alice had been seven. Her father had bought the house in order to get away from the scene of Queenie's accident, from dangerous vehicles, from potential encounters with disgruntled drivers. In those days, Alice loved to climb the elm trees and do cartwheels on the big front lawn or ride on the back of the gardener's mower through the maze of arborvitae with her brother Raymond. Now, she only went outside when she couldn't avoid it.

The phone rang as Alice was digging into her lunch. It was Aunt Rita.

"So, what the hell, Alice!" Rita said. "A call from the principal?"

"I got caught with some pot in my locker."

"I know that. How could you be so stupid? Who brings pot to school?" Rita, Alice's father's younger sister, could not have admonished her for smoking pot because Rita had been smoking pot for twenty years—since right after Kennedy was shot—and everyone knew it. Twice, she'd been kicked out of boarding school.

"I bought it at school. I was going to bring it home."

"Who's the bright guy selling pot at school?" Rita said.

"There are six dealers at my school," Alice said. She didn't add that she couldn't think of a more lucrative career for a teenager—Fox Grove was filled with kids who had money and nothing better to do than get high. What was unusual was the drug sweep. That was a first. Principal Altman said he planned to conduct more. What would that do to the Dustman's business? He'd have to move business off campus and sell it out of his house.

"Really? Six dealers?" Rita said. "That's bold."

"Are you going to tell my parents?" Alice said.

"I don't know," Rita said. "I think I have to."

"OK," Alice said.

"OK?"

"They won't give a shit anyway, Aunt Rita, and you know it," Alice said.

"What about Ray? Did you call him? He'd give you a talking to."

"He's too busy to care."

Her brother Ray was six years older and had been away at boarding school and college for many years. Before that, he was often a jerk, but he had taught Alice a lot. Her earliest memory was of him schooling her on bathroom hygiene.

"You wipe from front to back," he'd said, "until there's nothing left on the TP."

Ray was the one who'd taught her tennis and chess and even how to make paper airplanes and chocolate-chip cookie dough. He let her stay in his room when she saw monsters on the wall at night. For the past year he'd been working as a trader on Wall Street, though, and was too riled up to visit, or even to talk.

Later that afternoon, Alice called the Dustman. "They want to know who sold me the pot," she said.

"And you're not telling them, right? That would not be wise."

The Dustman had been Mike Gallagher until tenth grade when he smoked some marijuana laced with PCP. He thought he heard his mother calling to him from the rosemary topiary in the corner of the dining room, so he ran up to his room and leapt out of his bedroom window, thinking the hedge below looked soft as an air mattress. He walked away scraped up and covered in mulch and dirt. He never noticed the state of his attire and ended up wandering around town for several hours looking like an insane chimney sweep. Afterward, he didn't remember any of it, and had no idea why Alice, and soon everyone else, started calling him the Dustman.

More than just a steady hookup, the Dustman was Alice's best friend. They were together so much that their classmates would have called them a couple, but they had never classified the relationship or even referred to it at all. They hung out, they liked to get high, and sometimes they ended up in bed. Neither one of them had much faith in relationships, and both—though they hadn't acknowledged this to each other—were products of challenged parental units. If either had labeled it a commitment, it would have unnerved the other. Still, a day without seeing the Dustman was a bad day for Alice. He and her close friend, Missy Stewart, were the only two people she could bear to spend time with on a consistent basis.

"What should I do? If I don't tell them something, they're going to assume it was you. Plus, it's going to go on my record," Alice said.

"Why don't you make something up, Ollie. Say it was Lenny Brown or Gary Smith or one of those lowlifes. They're all dealing anyway . . ." Ollie was the Dustman's nickname for Alice. When they were getting high he liked to call, "Ollie Ollie oxen free," though neither one of them knew exactly what the saying meant.

"Are they?" Alice said. She had to agree that they looked like they might be dealing; scholarship students were suspicious by definition.

"Sure they are," the Dustman said. "Shit that'll make you cream. Especially Gary. That dude's tradin' some seriously funky juju. Do everybody a favor and turn that clown in."

"Maybe," Alice said.

"Plus, what about my dad? He could lose his job. That would be totally bogus."

The Dustman's father, Tom Gallagher, worked for Alice's father's tool-and-die manufacturing company. He'd been the acting president for the last six years since Mr. Townley had decided to retire and cruise the world. The news that the acting president's son had sold pot to the owner's daughter would not go over well with anyone. Besides that, Mike's mother was a local news anchor and famous in Detroit.

"OK," Alice said. "I'll do whatever you want."

"And listen," the Dustman said. "Since you're home and free as a bird, can you make a run for me? The muffler on my pickup fell off. Yesterday I got a ticket for disturbing the peace. I can't risk picking my next delivery up and getting pulled over. I'll spot you a four finger." He assured her that the location, 4235 New Hope Road, was only three miles from her house, and though the neighborhood looked like someone had taken a dump on it, everyone had moved out, so it was actually safer than it had ever been.

"No problem," Alice said.

When Missy called later that night she said that everyone at school was worried about the Dustman.

"Everybody buys from him," Missy said.

"I know," Alice said. "He said I should say it was Lenny or Gary or one of those retards."

"Say it was Gary; that guy's a douche bag. He sold a rancid Dutch to Cindy once, remember? She puked her guts out."

"Fine," Alice said. "I'll call tomorrow."

Alice went downstairs and scrounged through the cupboards in the kitchen looking for M&Ms. She'd been looking for her mother's stash the entire time her mother had been away, but she still hadn't found it. When Alice was little, this was a game she and her mother played. It took a long time to cover ten thousand square feet, and if her mother hid the candy well, the search might occupy Alice for most of an afternoon. These days her mother hid candy, not for Alice's benefit, but so she wouldn't undo the hours she'd put in on the tennis court with Dan, her tennis coach. She often forgot where she hid the bags, which meant that they were as liable to turn up in the garage as the TV room. Once Alice found them in the wrapping room under skeins of ribbon.

The next morning when Alice woke up at nine, there was a message from the Dustman on her answering machine saying that LaDonta, the dealer, would meet her at noon. Though the Dustman had assured her that the transaction would be safe and easy, Alice felt better knowing the dealer was a woman.

Alice went down to the kitchen, where Miss Powers was standing in front of the television watching *The Today Show* and drinking a cup of tea. Long or Dong came through with a bucket and mop and waved to Alice. She waved back and sat down at the counter. There was no way in hell she was driving her BMW into the ghetto.

"I'm meeting Rita for lunch," she said. "Can I borrow someone's car? Mine isn't working."

Miss Powers raised an eyebrow and smacked the dish towel against her thigh, but didn't question it. She said that Zhi-Yun Li had driven to work and she would ask her whether Alice could borrow her Pacer. Alice said she would fill it with gas in return.

Alice went out to the car with the directions the Dustman had given her and unlocked the door. The car was spotless—no trash, no dust or grime in between the bucket seats. The front seat had a cover on it that looked like shells woven together. It rolled this way and that when Alice sat down on it. When she pulled out of the driveway, she saw one of the cleaners—she assumed it was the one who had loaned her the car—wave at her from the side door.

"Thanks," she muttered. "I'll be so careful with your shit mobile, lady."

It was a straight shot to New Hope Road down MacArthur Avenue. A mile and a half from Alice's house, the suburbs ended and the city began. The minute Alice crossed the border, the leafy trees and impatiens disappeared, replaced with graffiti-covered buildings, homeless dogs, and scattered trash. Leaving the burbs, Alice's friends often joked, was like being expelled from Oz and reentering Kansas midtornado.

As Alice progressed down the street, she passed row upon row of dilapidated row houses. They all looked like they were on the verge of collapse, but the ones with people in them had mowed grass and bars on the windows. The others had broken glass and boards nailed over the doors. On the second block there were only two properties still standing on the left side and four on the right. The rest were fields and a garden someone had apparently started and then abandoned with a scarecrow slumped over on his pole and chicken wire around a thatch of weeds. The address was another block down. Alice, despite her earlier bravado, was nervous.

On the next block, Alice was surprised to see that an enormous compound—a castle-like Victorian house with a gated, run-down side yard—took up the entire left side of the road. She slowed to take a look at it. A sign over the front gate read: Mt. Carmel School for the Blind.

"That is fucked up," Alice said, noticing that there was also a temple of some sort across the street and a monk with a shaved head and bright-orange cloak was leaning over the side of a pond in the garden, tinkering with a hose.

At the end of the block on the right just beyond the temple was a line of four brick row houses. A black woman in jeans and a tight gray T-shirt was just coming down the front steps of the farthest house. Alice parked and got out of the car. The woman was tall, very broad across the shoulders, and very dark skinned. She was stuffed so tightly into her clothes that her stomach had busted out and hung like a flapjack over her jeans.

"LaDonta," she said. "Alice?"

When Alice nodded, LaDonta motioned to follow her up the front steps and into the house. Inside, a little girl of about four or five in Raggedy Ann pajamas sat watching *Tom and Jerry* on a dumpy, brown suede couch. She looked at them when they walked in and then quickly back at the TV. The TV surprised Alice because it was so large, blocking the whole fireplace. It looked out of place in the barren room, which contained only the couch and a card table with four chairs. LaDonta continued on through the room. At the kitchen door she stopped and asked Alice to sit down on the couch for a minute.

When Alice sat down, the little girl looked at Alice, her pink butterfly barrettes clacking.

"Is this your favorite show?" Alice said.

"No, *Scooby Doo*," the girl said, turning back to the TV.

"Me too!" Alice said. "But that wasn't around when I was a kid."

"What was?" the girl said, turning to her. Her eyes were huge and brown. Her mouth slanted down and Alice thought she looked sad and frightened, and then realized she might be thinking that because she was so afraid herself. Maybe the girl was just bored.

"My sister used to love *Tom and Jerry*, but I liked Bugs Bunny better." The minute she said it, she wondered why she had said it. The truth was, Queenie had hated cartoons. Instead she watched Shirley Temple movies, which came on TV every Sunday morning—but the bigger truth was that Alice couldn't be sure she wasn't making that memory up as well. It was hard to remember specific details about Queenie except that she liked to order Alice around and had been really cruel for a seven-year-old. One time she'd dragged Alice around by the hair, and another time she'd chased her around the yard hitting her over the head with a broom. It was one of the reasons Dr. Rich said Alice felt so much guilt—she hadn't liked her sister that much. And Queenie wasn't the only one Alice could say that about. It was true of her own mother. Alice could not remember her mother ever doing anything for her. She never bought Alice anything on her Christmas list, preferring instead to give her random items, most of which Alice recognized as regifts from the gift shelf in the wrapping room. Whenever she asked her mother to take her shopping or to the movies, her mother would say, "Sure, right after I get back from tennis," or "As soon as I take my walk." Again and again, Alice was the only one without a permission slip to go to the zoo or to the Cranbrook Museum, or the only one without any money in her cafeteria account, which would have required her mother remembering to send a check to the school. Her mother was never there for class parties or for Field Day. For a long time, Alice continued to hope her mother would show up. Then one day she just stopped hoping. Her father was OK when he was around, but he was hardly ever around. Seeing him was like bumping into her favorite waiter at Friendly's, good for a few minutes of mindless banter.

LaDonta returned and frowned at Alice. Alice wondered whether it was because she was talking to the little girl.

"See you," Alice said to the girl.

The kitchen was painted lavender. On the counter, there was a drying rack with several dishes in it. Aside from that there was nothing else on the counters or on the table. It smelled like bacon. Above the sink hung a picture of Jesus with a disappointed look on his face pointing at his own heart.

"What happened to the Dustman?" LaDonta said, going over to the window and looking out into the backyard. Alice was surprised at how silly the Dustman's name had sounded coming out of the woman's mouth.

"His car is fucked up," Alice said. She felt tough saying "fuck," like she was in a movie.

"Honey, what that? Watch your mouth! My daughter in there." LaDonta pointed to the door and shook her head.

"Sorry," Alice said.

"The usual?" LaDonta said, still standing with her back to Alice.

"Yes," Alice said. She realized the Dustman hadn't told her what she was picking up or how much it would cost. She had $300 on her. Was that enough? And what would happen if it wasn't?

LaDonta left the window, opened the avocado-colored oven, and extracted six baggies. She took them over to the table and set them down in front of Alice.

"Good?" she said. "Six here, quarter each, buck fifty total."

"Good," Alice said without looking at them. Thank God. One hundred fifty dollars. What a small, stupid amount. How much could the Dustman possibly be making? Alice wanted to leave, and fast.

"Tell him this shit better than last week."

"OK," Alice said. She counted out eight twenties. "Keep the change," she said.

"You leaving me a tip, Richie Rich?" LaDonta said. She smiled and Alice saw that she was missing her upper incisors, one on each side.

"Unless you have change?" Alice said.

"You didn't want change a minute ago." LaDonta folded the cash and crammed it into her jeans pocket.

Alice said nothing. Her face heated up and she realized she'd stopped breathing.

"How much you got on you anyway?" LaDonta said, coming closer, so close that Alice could smell the bacon on her breath. Her remaining teeth were yellow with black splotches in between.

Alice said nothing. She looked at the door.

"I'm messing with you, honey," LaDonta laughed, slapping Alice's shoulder. "You think I don't got change? I got change, but if you would like to leave me a tip I would take it, that's all I'm saying."

"OK," Alice said. "Keep it."

LaDonta's flip-flops made clacking noises as she walked over to a cupboard and pulled out a Cheerios box. She pulled the bag of cereal out of the box and placed the six baggies inside. Then she handed the box to Alice.

On the way out they passed through the living room again, but the little girl didn't respond when Alice said good-bye. When she and LaDonta reached the front door, Alice turned to her.

"What's that place across the street?" she said.

"School for blind people." LaDonta let out a whooping laugh. "They sure picked the right neighborhood!"

Back in the car, Alice put the cereal box on the passenger's seat and drove away as quickly as she could without actually peeling out.

Later, when she and the Dustman were sitting in her parents' private library on her mother's rose silk couch (just to spite her— because she would have had a cow), smoking and laughing at *The Cosby Show*, Alice asked him what the hell was wrong with him, going down to that part of town every week.

"Money's good," he said.

"Bullshit. You buy it for twenty-five dollars, you sell it for forty. That's crap. You don't need the money."

"Sure I do," he said, leaning closer to nibble on her ear. "You expect me to live on my allowance? Twenty bucks a week?"

"I don't know," Alice said, batting him away. "The whole time I was freaked out. That neighborhood sucks and LaDonta was scary. Doesn't seem worth it."

"Well, it's worth it," he said. "Someday I'm going to be a park ranger out west. I'm going to get the hell out of here and away from all these crappy neighborhoods. I'm saving up. I need money."

"You don't have to get away from those crappy neighborhoods," Alice said, running her hands through his powdery-white hair. "You don't even ever have to *go* there."

The Dustman shrugged and leaned in for a kiss.

Alice kissed him back. "Why do you want to be a park ranger?" she said after a moment.

"People. Don't like them. But I'm all for mountains and nature. And I like the idea of living all by myself in a cabin in the woods."

"Like a hermit," Alice said.

"Yup, but you're welcome to come along, Ollie." He got up from the couch and headed over toward the bathroom.

"Not a chance," Alice said.

"To be a park ranger I have to take a two-year training course, and to do that, I have to graduate from high school. Get my drift?" He punched the part of the wall that looked like paneling but was really a secret door to the bathroom. "I love this fucking door," he said.

The next morning Alice called Principal Altman. "It was Gary Smith," she said.

At school on Monday, Alice felt like a hero. Nobody liked Gary anyway. He had an attitude problem. He never talked to anyone, always sat alone. At lunch, Missy said she was glad he was gone. He was a psycho. He'd practically snapped her head off when she asked if he had some pot. "You think because I'm black, I'm a drug dealer?" he'd said.

"So he doesn't deal?" Alice said. "I thought you said he did."

"He was a scholarship kid," Missy said. "Duh . . ."

"Duh, what?" Alice said. She didn't know if that meant of course he was dealing because he was poor or black or of course he wasn't because he needed the scholarship.

"He was an asshole," Missy said. "One of those 'I'm too good for you' assholes. Well, you know what I have to say to that? Good fucking luck, fucker."

On Friday morning Alice's parents called. They were sorry they hadn't checked in earlier, but they had decided to cross from the Caribbean to the Med and they'd gotten caught in a storm that lasted two days.

"Two days I couldn't even stand up!" her father said. "Swells must have been forty feet high. Your mother was crying and crying. I had to give her two Valiums and then we actually had to strap her to the bed so she wouldn't roll out."

When he asked what was new, Alice said nothing.

"Well, we'll be home a little later than we thought—probably a week from Friday," he said. "Can't wait to see you."

After she hung up, the phone rang again, so fast she figured it was her father who'd forgotten something. "Yeah?" she said.

"Why?" a voice said.

"Who is this?" Alice said, even though she knew.

"Why'd you do that to me? Why'd you lie?"

"What?"

"You ruined my life."

Alice hung up. Her heart was pounding. It had to be Gary. Why would he call her? He had to know he'd get caught at some point. All she'd done was speed up the outcome.

She went over to the bedside table and opened the drawer. After she smoked a joint she felt better. How could she turn the Dustman in? She couldn't. What had happened to Gary was unfortunate, but a person had to have loyalties.

She picked up the phone and called her brother Ray.

"What?" he yelled into the phone. Alice wondered whether he always yelled into the phone and, if so, what his clients thought of it. He always did it to her and she hated it.

"It's Alice. I have to talk to you."

"Not a good time, Al."

"It's really, really important."

"Hit me. Two minutes. Go."

"I got caught with pot. The Dustman sold it to me. I couldn't rat him out, so I said it was this other kid and the kid got kicked out."

"The other kid was a dealer too?"

"No. Well, I'm not sure. I thought so. He's a scholarship student."

"Ow! That's low! That's really low."

"So what do I do?"

"Are you going to turn the Dustman in?"

"No."

"Well, then I'm not sure what you can do. I'm a little surprised at you, Al. I thought you learned your lesson last year."

Last year when her parents were away, Alice had thrown a party in the boathouse and Reenie McCall had fallen asleep with a lit cigarette. They'd all barely made it out of the structure before it was consumed in flames, and then only because the Dustman had been playing the Pink Floyd album. Instead of "Get Your Filthy Hands Off My Desert," the Dustman, who had become obsessed with the song, liked to scream "Get Your Filthy Hands Off My Dessert." That night the song's incoming bomb sequence had roused a girl named Amy Enders, who had screamed bloody murder and woken them all up. Because it was dark and all of her friends had arrived on boats, no one had been able to prove the fire had anything to do with Alice, though her father had made a point of saying that he didn't know many "intruders" who arrived by speedboat. This year her father had padlocked the newly constructed boathouse before he left and given the key to Miss Powers, who was only to open it if Alice was supervised.

On Saturday morning Miss Powers announced that she was taking the night off, going to stay with her sister who was flying through town on her way to Chicago. They'd have one night together, Miss Powers said, and one night was plenty. Since Long and Dong were off for the weekend, the only one who could stay and look after Alice was Mr. Richardson.

"Tell him to forget it," Alice said to Miss Powers. "I don't need him looking after me."

Miss Powers stood next to the side door with what looked like a little black doctor's bag by her feet. She shook her head. "Your parents said some adult has to be here. I'm sorry. You know he won't bother you one bit. He'll just stay in his room the whole time watching the telly."

"I hope so," Alice said. He hadn't done it so far but Alice had the feeling that one day when she passed him in the hall he was going to grab her wrist or put his hand on her ass. He had that leering look about him. Her parents couldn't care less; in a pinch they would leave her with *anyone.*

"I hope he doesn't say one fucking word to me," Alice added.

Miss Powers tsked. "Watch your mouth, little lady," she said, wagging her finger. Alice turned away.

As soon as Miss Powers's car had disappeared down the driveway, Alice called the Dustman. There was no fucking way she was staying home alone with Mr. Richardson.

"I'm having a party tonight," she said, knowing he would get the word out. She'd promised her father no more parties but fuck him. Being left alone with Mr. Richardson was the last straw.

That night, Alice waited until she was sure her friends were en route before knocking on Mr. Richardson's door. She didn't want to get stuck talking to him for more than five minutes tops.

"Come in," he called.

Alice hesitated before opening the door. When she did, she pushed it open without actually stepping inside the room. Mr. Richardson was on his mud-brown comforter in his boxers and T-shirt, drinking a Milwaukee's Best and watching television. The bed was facing the TV. He didn't look over at her; he kept his eyes glued to the television. Alice felt sick looking at him in the bed, a grown man—an old, fat man of fifty or more—in his underwear.

"I'm having a few friends over," she said. "We won't be loud. I just wanted you to know."

"No problem," Mr. Richardson said. He kept his eyes on the TV, but his hand, she noticed, was in his boxer shorts. Alice felt her stomach heave.

"Just don't burn the house down this time," he said.

"OK," she said, reaching in and pulling the door closed with a resounding thwack.

The party that night was a party that kids talked about for years afterward. Alice unlocked the liquor cabinet and the wine cellar. Neil Wilbur, one of the varsity linebackers, hatcheted through the padlock on the boathouse door. Alice snuck into the room next to Mr. Richardson's and into his bathroom. She unplugged his phone and locked the door to the third-floor staircase. He wouldn't realize he was trapped unless he actually tried to get out. Partygoers lowered the two speedboats into the water. They put up the sails on the catamaran. The moon was full and the light rippled through the elm trees. Unlike other neighborhood parties, the Townley Estate was large enough and the street far enough away that no one was fearful of the police. All of the cars parked around the circular drive and down in the back by the boathouse were shielded by the arborvitae. Sometimes noise echoed off the water, but that night the wind was in their favor and the sound rippled out across the Detroit River toward Windsor. There were kids in every elm tree, kids in every room of the house, kids in speedboats cruising at high speed up and down the river. Alice, the Dustman, and a couple of other kids took mushrooms and did cartwheels across the grass. They trained a spotlight on the lake and watched the fish glittering under the black water; they passed a bottle of vodka and flicked their cigarette butts all over the lawn. Later on the Dustman put in a French movie, which he promised was better than porn, and a large group of kids crashed on the sofas in the basement. At one point a boy got up to go to the bathroom and veered into a framed autograph that F. Scott Fitzgerald had given to Alice's grandmother, which read, "No, Mrs. Townley, you absolutely may not have my autograph."

"No big deal," Alice said when he started picking up the shattered glass. "Just leave it there."

Alice's phone rang. It was Missy, who was home with a cold.

"Man," Alice said. "You picked the worst night to be sick."

"Alice," Missy said. "I have some crazy news."

The Dustman tapped Alice and handed her a straw. She leaned in to do the lines he'd laid out for her on the table.

"That kid Gary just got fished out of the Detroit River," Missy said.

Alice, midsnort, inhaled so quickly she felt the burn through her whole nose.

"Fell in the Detroit River," Missy said.

"Dead?" Alice said.

"I think some guy in a speedboat rescued him just in time," Missy said. "I guess he got lucky."

"Lucky," Alice said.

Lucky.

When his son left, Ralph's nightmares revved up. The artillery chattered again after more than fifty years détente. Several times a week, Ralph woke up in the middle of the street or crouched on the sidewalk. Getting up, he would stand for several minutes heaving, his heart ratcheting around in his chest. Frozen, straining to listen, he could make out only an occasional car horn above the rustle of the willow tree in the front yard. After a few minutes he would relax, noting that all of the houses were dark and none of the neighborhood pets were keening or barking.

If there had been an alarm, it had sounded for him alone.

On the last day of Frank's visit, he'd announced that the long trips to Bay City were too difficult to coordinate with his children's numerous sports commitments. He strongly suggested that his father move south to Asheville, going as far as to say that he had time off in August, and if Ralph had the house sold by then, he would be more than willing to help him pack. In the meantime he would find a small apartment for Ralph near his own house, perhaps in Long Meadows, the tiny assisted-living center that, for a premium, offered mountain views.

"I know it's tough to leave home," Frank said when Ralph balked. "But I think it makes sense for a number of reasons."

Ralph had to acknowledge that Frank was right. He was eighty-one years old and his family lived a thousand miles away. He contacted a real-estate broker who used to play bridge with his wife, Adrienne.

The next day, Dede Andrews arrived in a red BMW and clicked through the ranch in three-inch heels, pausing only to test a water faucet or jiggle open a jammed closet door. As she trotted through the rooms, which had not been papered or painted for more than ten years, she clapped her hands and chirped, "Charming!" "Moldings!" Running her hand over the red Naugahyde bench in the breakfast nook, she pronounced it "Vintage!" and gave a vigorous nod of approval.

"Well, the street's iffy, as you know," she said as Ralph followed her back to the car. "But the house has charm."

When they reached the car, Dede turned to Ralph and took hold of his hand.

"This is going to be hard, honey, but you need to declutter. I think you should clean out the closets and the basement, if you can. It will look like you have more space, and more space, more money . . . I'm sure you wouldn't mind that."

Ralph's street, Edgemere Lane, contained an odd conflagration of duplexes and smaller homes. It was a hot spot for people upended—the newly divorced, single mothers and their children, the occasional disabled person who favored the first-floor flats and the wheelchair ramps installed by previous tenants. People raved about Edgemere's proximity to the village boutiques and bagel shops, but most Bay City residents gravitated toward traditional streets with two-car garages, one-family homes, and quiet, fenced-in yards. Every now and then a newly married couple moved in, but for the most part it was a place for people more permanently displaced. Ralph and Adrienne had moved there initially to save money, but after a few years Ralph realized he appreciated the transience of the other residents—how unlikely they were to notice his own eccentricities.

The only neighbor Ralph knew well, even after fifteen years, was Lauren Gallagher. Lauren lived in the duplex next door to Ralph and Adrienne's small ranch. Lauren's husband, the assistant district attorney, had been shot outside a crack house in Detroit. According to the paper, he had been a frequent customer.

Lauren, looking bitter and confused, had carted all of their expensive French provincial furniture, the silver and crystal, down from her six-bedroom house on Mapleton to the left side of 453 Edgemere. It turned out her husband had squandered most of their money on drugs, so Lauren had answered an ad for a job taking care of an agoraphobic woman who lived in the right side of the duplex. The job required she check on Estelle Warner three times a day and shop for any supplies she might need. In return Lauren received a small stipend and free rent.

She had managed Estelle's care ever since. It had seemed like the perfect short-term solution for a woman in her early sixties who had never worked and whose only child was grown, but in many ways Ralph felt it had been her undoing. She had never met another man, trapped as she was in her insular routine, and the job had proved never-ending. Estelle, nearly ninety now, was as cushioned and cozy as a fetus in the womb. She never seemed to age or sicken.

Lauren's only real joy was her grandson, Mike, who came up from Detroit to stay every summer. Lauren's daughter-in-law was a television news anchor and her hectic schedule made her largely unavailable for Mike, even in the summer months. Lauren's son Tom ran a manufacturing company of some sort. He was determined, according to Lauren, not to follow in his own father's footsteps, and he worked around the clock.

Ralph had seen a lot of Lauren and her grandson Mike in the early days, when Mike had helped Ralph and Adrienne out in the perennial garden and decorated sugar cookies at the tiny kitchen table. He had brought them both a lot of joy in the days after Frank was long gone, and the possibility of grandchildren seemed remote.

The day after Dede's inspection, Ralph started clearing out the guest room. After all, he reasoned, cleaning out the least-used room was like tiptoeing into the shallow end instead of diving into the pool. But it was not as easy as he thought. The room was filled to the brim; Adrienne had been a collector. Conchshell collection on the windowsills, bookshelves lining every wall, filled with Tarot card boxes and hundreds of gardening books. In a box in the top of the closet, he found his father's prayer missal and homemade fishing lures, which Adrienne must have squirreled away soon after they bought the house.

When he opened the missal, several Mass cards spilled out onto the floor. His hand shook as he picked them up. He placed them in a cardboard box by his feet on which he'd marked "save" in black magic marker. Farther down in the box was a set of lace doilies, yellowed with age, which his mother had fashioned. He put them on the bed to label them. Someday when Ralph was gone, Frank was sure to mistake them for rags. Next came an old Carlisle Allen jewelry box, and inside that some love letters he had written to Adrienne when they were courting. It took a moment of close scrutiny before he recognized the wobbly, adolescent handwriting. He carried the box over to the bed, and sat down.

There were, it turned out, only four letters on top of a pile of poems. He picked up the first poem. The opening line read: "I am a whirling dervish." Ralph laughed out loud. Adrienne had dabbled in poetry very briefly in her midforties, but later pooh-poohed the rhymes as stacks of "hormonally charged fluff."

He could not bring himself to read the letters. He put down the poem and walked out of the room, leaving the bureau drawers open and detritus from the box scattered across the bed. It looked like CIA operatives had ransacked the room. In the kitchen he poured a glass of milk and went out on the back porch to play solitaire.

That night the rain brought him around. In the first disoriented minutes the water dripping on his face felt like baby fingers tapping on his nose. He was lying face up on the sidewalk, his arms and legs wide open. He rolled onto his side and sat up slowly, looking up and down the street. There wasn't a sound beside the patter of the rain.

Getting up, he suddenly felt off-balance and reached for a nearby elm tree to steady himself. His knee ached, and he stretched his leg. A light blinked on at the Gallaghers' house. It was the front-right light, the one in Estelle's bathroom. A lace curtain covered the window, but he could just make out the shadow of a figure standing behind it, peering out at the street. Then the shadow moved away and the light went out.

Had she heard him? Had he yelled? If he had, wouldn't other people have emerged from their houses? He glanced around, but there was no one.

He had never met Estelle, but from what Lauren had told him, she was a tiny, waif-like woman who spent most of her time on the couch, knitting and watching Christian television. The only time Lauren had ever seen her agitated was ten years before when she'd suffered from appendicitis. Lauren had had to take her to the hospital and the minute Lauren drove out of the attached garage, Estelle had gone catatonic and hadn't said a word or responded to anyone until she returned to her house a week later.

"She just shut down," Lauren said. "It was almost like she ceased to exist. If I hadn't been there, the doctors would have had no idea it was an appendicitis. She wasn't even responsive enough to point to her side. I have never met someone so paralyzed by the world."

"I know what that's like," Ralph had told Adrienne later that night when they were sitting on the porch.

"I know you do," she said.

"I mean the terror part. Not the hiding out."

"I know."

"It probably doesn't even work." He'd meant the seclusion. He didn't think it would help, hiding out in the house. What sanctuary is a house when you're running from yourself? During his evening strolls, it always made him sad to pass her house and see the white wicker rocking chair on the porch swaying in the breeze.

After Ralph had changed into dry clothes and poured himself a glass of milk, he opened the drawer next to the phone and pulled out a pad of paper. Initially he was writing to apologize for his behavior, but as he penned the note it occurred to him that she might be able to empathize with his plight.

Estelle:

I am sorry if I have disturbed you, but I have been troubled by nightmares (war related) which have started up again for some unknown reason but should resolve soon. I am moving to Asheville in August.

Sincerely,

Ralph Williams

The first months after the war had been horrific. It was as if during all the fighting and chaos he had been in shock, and when he came home he was forced to relive every moment accompanied by the terror he should have felt the first time around. He would be in the Village Diner or in Woolworth's eating an egg sandwich, and without any warning he was in New Guinea again, lying flat in the jungle thicket, a piece of shrapnel in his chest, his feet splayed, listening, terrified, to the gunfire resounding above him. When these visions came on him, he would leave the money on the counter and stumble out onto the sidewalk, the artillery louder than the traffic on the street. Then he would walk along the tree-lined streets until it subsided because at least when he was moving he couldn't feel the trembling in his limbs. Falling into bed at night, he would be roused by the "ack-ack" of machine guns so loud he bit right through his tongue one night and woke up with blood on his undershirt. Whatever this was, it had him round the neck, and it gripped so tight that one day he stuck his hand up into the attic aperture and pulled out the Japanese 38 rifle he'd hidden there.

The thing that stopped him from putting it in his mouth was the thought of his parents' shame. They had lived through enough already—a daughter who died of rheumatic fever in '36, and then the uncertainty of two sons at war. Another thing that got him was pride. Weren't all of his friends adjusting? Danny Renton and Steve Smith spent every night at the Vogue Lounge, listening to Benny Goodman, smoking Kents, and drinking Manhattans. They joked around like two chums who had never wandered any farther than Main Street. It wasn't until Nixon was impeached that Steve admitted he'd slept in the bathtub for months after the war.

In the early years, Ralph's mother always heard him bounding down the stairs. She was the one who led him, dismayed and tearful, back into the house every night. After a cup of warm Ovaltine, she would sit on the edge of his bed, running her fingers through his hair while he clenched and unclenched his fists.

Then one day he ran into Adrienne at Field's Market; she was his best friend Stan's younger sister. After that, the dreams dried up, the sirens receded. He thought it was gone forever.

❧

The following day, Dede called to say that she had several people who wanted to see the house. When could he have it ready?

"That depends on what you mean by ready," Ralph said. He was standing in the kitchen looking out onto the backyard. A squirrel was wrestling with a bag of Better Made potato chips.

"Well, Ralph, that's up to you. If you clear everything out, I'm going to push for more money. If not, I'm going to have to take that into account."

If he had to move to Asheville, he might as well have a mountain view.

It was Thursday. "I'll have it cleaned out by Sunday," he said.

"Are you sure?"

When Ralph said he was, she said she would bring her clients over at 9:00 a.m. on Monday.

Ralph poured a glass of iced tea and took it out onto the porch. It was very hot outside. He sat down at the beveled-glass table and shuffled his cards. How was he ever going to get it done by Sunday? The guest room was still in complete disarray. He hadn't done anything for three days. As he laid the cards out on the table, he heard someone yell.

"You get out there and do it! I'm telling you, if you don't have it done by noon, you'll be sorry!"

Lauren was sparring with Mike. He'd arrived the week before and they were already at it. When he was little, they'd gotten along beautifully, but the last few years had seemed more contentious. Ralph wasn't sure whether Mike was in the grip of normal teenage angst or there was something more sinister going on. It seemed possible that he felt neglected because of his mother's busy schedule. In all the years that Mike had been visiting, Ralph had only met his mother Susan once. Normally she commissioned someone else to drive Mike up for the summer.

The back door slammed and Mike loped out into the yard. Black pants, black T-shirt, spiked bracelets up both sides of his arms. White hair jutted out from his head like the spokes on a wheel. His skin was so white it looked like he was wearing lipstick. Ralph watched as he went over to the garden shed in the back of the yard, unlatched the door, and started his long, desultory march across the backyard, the lawn mower humming. He had to be burning up in that outfit.

Ralph played solitaire until the humming subsided. Then he pushed open the screen door and started across the lawn. Mike was putting the mower back in the shed. Ralph waved to him and Mike grimaced as if he were facing a dentist wielding a drill.

"How are you?" Ralph held out his hand. Mike looked at it and raised one of his jeweled arms in a brief, staccato wave.

"Listen, I've got a note for Estelle, if you'd give it to her." Ralph handed him the note. Mike snatched it and jammed it into his pocket.

"I've also got a job here." He pointed toward the house. "I've got to clean this place out. I'm moving down south near Frank and I've got to get all this junk out by Sunday. Do you want to earn some money?"

"What do I have to do?" Mike still hadn't smiled. How was it possible to be so young and healthy and miserable?

"Well, I thought I'd box up all the stuff I want and then you can box up the rest and put it in a pile for Goodwill."

"How much are you paying?"

Brother, Ralph thought. "Five dollars an hour," he said.

"I'll think it over." Mike turned back toward his house. Ralph went inside and picked up the cards. A few minutes later he looked up to see Lauren crossing the yard. He got up and opened the door for her.

"Ralph, how are you?" She gave him a light kiss on the cheek and a mild squeeze for a hug. She had grown old over the last couple of years. When she first moved in next door, she had been quite attractive—she'd kept her figure and her hair was always nicely arranged. Now it was white and frizzy. She wore no makeup. When she smiled, wrinkles fanned out like starbursts from the corners of her eyes.

"I saw you talking to Mike, but he wouldn't tell me what it was about. I thought I'd come over and make sure he didn't say anything deranged. It's like he thinks he's Dracula or the Antichrist. I don't know what's the matter with him these days." She was trying to joke about it, but she sounded like a chemotherapy patient making light of hair loss.

"I offered him a job," Ralph said, explaining that Frank had talked him into moving south.

She put her hand to her mouth. "I'm going to miss you," she said. As she grabbed his arm, he remembered her face when he'd told her Adrienne had passed away—as if she'd lost the one thing holding her up. Adrienne had been a friend to her during the first tough years on Edgemere following her husband's scandalous death, when most of her own family had abdicated. The lack of activity at Lauren's house over the last few years suggested that she hadn't established many other firm connections since Adrienne died, and he felt sorry for her.

"Maybe I didn't offer him enough money."

"He'll take anything he can get," she said. "He'll be here tomorrow morning. What time do you want him?"

Ralph asked if eight would be too early, and Lauren laughed.

"Oh, Ralph, I'll be delighted to wake him up at eight." She pushed open the screen door and stepped back out into the yard. "And if he's his usual surly self, don't let it bother you. Just tell him what to do and let me know if he gives you any lip. I'll take care of it."

That night Ralph woke up at the front door. The humidity always caused the door to stick, and the effort of yanking it open had roused him out of his dream. His heart ached. He managed to get the door open and he stepped onto the front stoop for some air. Standing there shaking, he wondered how long he could go on like this before he had a heart attack. He walked down the steps to the sidewalk and stopped, breathing deeply, trying to calm down. He checked his watch. It was 2:15 a.m.

He was pacing up and down several minutes later trying to steady his breath when a car rounded the corner and hurtled down the street right toward him. For a minute Ralph thought it might hit him, but it passed by and screeched to a stop in front of the Gallaghers'. The driver was Mike in Lauren's junky old Chevette. He turned off the engine and sat in the car listening to loud, thwunking music and blowing smoke out the window. Finally, a couple of minutes later, he emerged. Ralph thought about waving or calling, "Hello," but Mike never looked at him. He stumbled up the path to his house with his eyes on the ground. It took him a long time to fit the key in the lock and open it.

"He's going to be a big help tomorrow," Ralph muttered, as the door clicked shut.

Looking around as he always did for signs of life, he noticed that Estelle's light was on again. She must have heard the car. He turned toward the window, but as he did so the curtain rustled and the light went out.

"Good night, dear lady," he called to the dark house.

Ralph had trouble getting out of bed the next morning, but he had awakened with a renewed sense of determination. He would get the job done. Then he would move south to Long Meadows, where there was bound to be at least one decent gin-rummy player.

Attitude is everything, he reminded himself as he buttered his toast.

After breakfast, he went up to the guest bedroom and opened the door. The scene frightened him, but he steeled himself, and by midmorning he had extracted every significant memento from the pile of rubbish. It was just after eleven when he heard someone calling loudly from the screen porch.

It was Mike, wearing his ghoulish black pants and shirt, replete with black combat boots. Looking closer, Ralph noted the pale skin, the dark circles, the white-blond hair in disarray. He was standing on the porch, sporting his distinctive angry scowl.

"Thanks for coming," Ralph said. "I just finished the guest room. You can start in there. I've got lots of boxes from Kroger. Just put everything neatly in the boxes and mark 'giveaway' on the side. If you come across anything you want, just take it."

Mike looked at him as if that idea was ludicrous.

Ralph spent the remainder of the morning in his own room going through his desk. In one drawer he found a pile of old

Christmas cards. Flipping through, he was astonished by the number of people he had completely forgotten about or simply lost touch with. He spent another hour rifling through random pictures, pausing for a long time to study one of Adrienne taken right before she got sick. She was sitting at the tiki bar at the Bitter End Yacht Club. "May the next twenty-five years be so sunny the Caribbean will pale in comparison," she'd said in her toast that night.

Around one in the afternoon, he decided to take a break for lunch. On his way downstairs, he stopped by the guest room and knocked lightly on the door. No sound. He put his hand on the knob and turned it. Inside, Mike was asleep on the twin bed by the closet. It looked like he had one box half packed.

At first, Ralph thought about taking the table lamp and bashing him over the head. But then Mike snored lightly and turned over, curling up on his side. He slept with his hands tucked under his head and his mouth open, his eyelashes long and curly like a girl's. For the first time Ralph noticed how skinny he was—his leg bone outlined underneath the black pants looked like a tire iron jutting out from his hip. Sleeping, he might have been the most contented person on earth. It occurred to Ralph that if the situation was reversed and someone happened in on him, they would not witness such peaceful slumber. It would be a sin to disturb it. He shut the door and went downstairs to make lunch.

While he fixed his bologna sandwich he wondered what had happened to Mike. After Adrienne died, he stopped coming by every day in the summer. She had been the draw. He was eleven then, just beginning to let his hair grow, just beginning to shuffle and smirk. There were afternoons when Ralph, playing solitaire at the table, had spotted smoke rising up behind the toolshed where several sloppy neighborhood kids were clustered. Couldn't Lauren see them from the kitchen? Why didn't she roust them out? Perhaps it was simply a phase, he'd decided at the time. After all, hadn't he smoked in the alley when he was a boy? Since then, however, the clothes, the hair, and the music all seemed to signal a much more ominous transformation. Perhaps she didn't want to come down hard on him when their time together every year was so brief.

He left a bologna sandwich on the table and returned to his room, where he worked diligently all afternoon, telling himself that he was excavating an ancient ruin and the artifacts should mean no more to him than they would to any other dispassionate archaeologist.

At 5:00 p.m. he knocked on the bedroom door. Getting no answer, he opened it and found the room empty. There were only three boxes packed, barely a dent made in the whole mess. No one was in the kitchen. The bologna sandwich was gone. An empty Coke can remained overturned in the sink. That night, playing solitaire on the porch, Ralph kept an eye on the house next door. The only person he saw was Lauren, who made a brief appearance in the kitchen window before turning out the lights.

He slept fitfully but never ventured out into the street. He did not think Mike would come back the following day, but around ten the screen door slammed.

"Hey," Mike said when Ralph poked his head out of the bedroom. He was standing with his hand on the guest-room door. "I didn't finish," he said.

"I'm glad to see you," Ralph said.

"What do I do after I'm done in there?"

It seemed extremely unlikely that Mike would finish in the guest room, but Ralph said that he could start in on his bedroom afterward.

"I've got most of my stuff out of here," Ralph said. "You can pack the giveaway boxes and I'll move down to the living room."

"Okeydokey." Mike slipped into the guest room.

Ralph had remained tolerably detached the day before, and had convinced himself he could handle anything that surfaced, which was why he was so surprised to feel his heart clench when he came across the shoe box in the bottom of the closet. It was crammed in the back, underneath a pile of shoes. Inside he found the black box. He touched the small gold clasp, and it popped open.

He had not seen the medals since January 1946. He did not remember moving them from the old house to the new one. Had Adrienne done it?

Opening the box was like falling into a mass grave. The Bronze Star, Colin Mayhew, New Guinea, a bayonet wound, his eyes, the way they glazed over, the last few minutes, dying wall-eyed on Ralph's lap. Later in the Philippines, the whole squadron ambushed by the Japanese on the road to Baguio. Thirty men dead (Mick Tompkins, his best friend among them) before Filipino guerrillas burst out of the jungle and saved the rest.

Ralph placed the medals on his desk and hurried out of the room. He went downstairs and lay down on the divan in the living room. When he woke up, Mike was standing over him.

"I'm done," he said. "I'll see you tomorrow."

"Right," Ralph said. "I guess I fell asleep here." He sat up and rubbed his face, feeling old and silly.

"Yeah," Mike said, attempting a smile that looked more like a scowl. "See ya."

"You're keeping track of your hours?"

"Sure."

That night Ralph met up with all of his old cronies. Colin was sitting on a tree stump fashioning a stick pipe. Tommy was smoking, lounging under a banyan on the beach in Luzon. As he embraced them and laughed with delight, each one melted in his arms like so much sand. He awoke on the sidewalk. He was kneeling, doubled over, his head near the cement. There was a hand on his back. He looked up to find Mike leaning over him, a cigarette dangling from his lips.

"Man, you were praying so loudly, I could hear you before I opened the car door," Mike said. "You were like yelling, 'Jesus, Mary, and Joseph!' I'm surprised my grandma's not out here."

"How embarrassing," Ralph said. He put a hand up over his eyes. His whole face was wet.

"What's the matter, Mr. Williams?" Mike said.

"Please don't tell your grandmother."

"No, I won't, but you ought to go to the doctor or something. Man, that was weird."

It occurred to him that Mike was describing what he had just witnessed the way a person might detail the behavior of an indigenous tribesman on a National Geographic special—as if he couldn't relate to it at all.

Mike helped him up and Ralph stood for a minute with his hands on his hips to steady himself. He looked down the street and noted, with a shock, that Estelle's front door was open.

"Wow," Mike muttered. "That's a first."

She was as small as a prepubescent girl. She wore a shroud or some sort of floor-length housedress. He could just make out a cloud of white hair piled up in a bun on top of her head before she scuttled out of sight, shutting the door softly. She had clearly watched the whole scene unfold. If Mike hadn't appeared, would she have come to his rescue? Would she have ventured through the door? What would it have cost her to cross that threshold? She had looked prepared to do it. Sitting at the kitchen table later, with a glass of warm milk steaming beside him, Ralph wrote another note of apology.

Dear Estelle:

> Perhaps you are concerned about me.
> For the most part, I am OK. Just an old soldier who thinks he's still at war. Hope you are well.

> Sincerely,

> Ralph Williams

The next morning Mike showed up at eight thirty. Ralph gave him the note, which he said he would slip under Estelle's door at lunch. During the day Mike actually smiled once and Ralph wondered whether he hadn't started to appreciate his own relative good fortune after bearing witness to an old man's malaise.

Midafternoon, as Ralph was cleaning out a bookshelf in the living room, Mike came down with the black box.

"I think you left this in the room by mistake," he said. "I'm sure you want to keep these."

"I'm not sure." Ralph stood up.

Mike opened the box and held it out to Ralph. Ralph kept his eyes on Mike's face.

"They're so cool." Mike knelt down next to the coffee table. He fingered the medals, pulling them out one by one. "The Purple Heart! That's big, man. If you don't want them, can I have them?" He laid them out one by one on the table.

"No!" Ralph yelled. He sank down onto the couch, his hands over his face. His palms were wet, his mouth chalky.

"Sorry," Mike said, backing away. "You left them there. I could have put them in a giveaway box by mistake."

"I didn't mean to yell. It's just that only the soldier who earns them can wear them. It's a rule."

"Oh." Mike shrugged. He headed for the stairs.

"Otherwise, I'd give them to you," Ralph added in apology.

"Maybe I'll get that chance," Mike called over his shoulder.

"What?"

Mike turned around, his hand on the banister.

"I might enlist," he said. "They need help over in the Middle East."

"What about your grandmother? What about your parents?"

"I'm not quite old enough, but by the time I am, believe me, they'll all be happy to see me go." A corner of his mouth lifted.

"You know, I'd think of that as the last option," Ralph said. He almost added, "It's not something you do because you don't know what else to do," but he didn't really think Mike was serious about enlisting and, if he was, he didn't want him taking offense and storming out before they were done packing.

"What do you really want to do with your life?" Ralph said.

"It's dumb," Mike said. "I won't do it."

Mike rubbed a cross into the dust of one of the giveaway boxes. "I want to be a park ranger. You know, roam around outside. Away from the world. No stuff. You know?"

Ralph looked at him. He looked like he was serious. "Well, if you want to do that, you should do it."

"My mom would have a cow."

"Is it her life?" Ralph said.

"I guess not," Mike said. "But the military . . . she would think that was much cooler."

"You could get hurt," Ralph said. "She wouldn't like that."

"Yeah," Mike said, but he didn't sound sure of it.

That night he paid Mike $200, far more than he had offered. Perhaps he would take it as a token of his affection.

"Good luck, Mr. Williams," he said, cramming the money into his pocket.

"You too." They were standing in front of the screen door facing each other. Ralph was suddenly struck with a vision of himself at that same age. They were exactly the same height. He'd once had the same soft, translucent skin, not even the shadow of a beard. Without thinking he took hold of Mike's bony shoulders and pulled him close. The boy flinched underneath Ralph's grip, which was firm.

"Be a park ranger. Being a hero is not a happy business," Ralph whispered into his ear.

Ralph and Mike had stored all of the Goodwill boxes in the garage. On Monday Dede brought her first clients through. On Tuesday a fat, affable young man with a turquoise cross in his left earlobe came and loaded all twenty-seven boxes onto the truck. The nightmares seemed to happen with less frequency after that.

Two weeks later Dede found a buyer, a musician named Mel who had spent the last twenty years teaching band at the high school. The closing date was set for the end of August. That summer, with more time on his hands, Ralph wandered through town, saying good-bye to all of his old haunts. He was surprised not to feel more nostalgic. As he was sitting on a bench outside of Dave's Haircutting Shop, he was reminded of something Adrienne had said a couple of weeks before she died. She was in the hospital then. A nurse had just brought in breakfast. She could no longer eat so she motioned for Ralph to take the tray.

"You know, I was sitting here early this morning and this small, wiry guy limps into the room and he's changing the orange Hefty bag in that trash can, and I just start talking to him, asking him where he's from, how he likes working at the hospital, how long he's been here, just chatting really. He's as nice as can be, and when he's finished he comes over, sits down on the bed, and takes my hand. He looks me right in the eye, and says, 'I'm so sorry.'"

"Sorry for what?" Ralph almost said. He wanted to pretend he didn't know what she meant, but her eyes had filled, and he didn't have the strength for it.

She cleared her throat. "So I said, 'How did you know?' and he says, 'The other patients don't pay any attention to me.'"

At the time Ralph had been more dismayed by her tears than by the story. But now he understood it completely. Sitting on the bench, he watched the women with their strollers, the business-men in suits, the children on their bicycles, the teenagers sashaying into the bagel store. No one except those who know how fleeting it is pay any attention at all.

One night about a week before Frank arrived to pick him up, Ralph woke up in the middle of the night. It suddenly seemed perfectly clear to him. He picked up the medals, walked down the stairs, and opened the front door. The night was hot and humid. The garbage cans were lined up along the street where he'd placed them. Standing in front of them, he opened the box one last time. For a moment, with the streetlight shining down on it, the burnished gold around the Purple Heart seemed to glow. He snapped the lid, glancing anxiously around.

No one was there, except Estelle in her bathroom. A little bun peeked out over the lace curtain like a rabbit face. He turned away from the garbage can and faced her. She didn't move. What seemed like an hour passed. Ralph's knee started to throb. A new plan presented itself. He started a swift march toward her house. The little bun dipped beneath the lace curtain and the light blinked out. Still he forged ahead, up the stairs onto the porch. Opening the screen door, he bent down so that his mouth was next to the mail slot.

"My dear lady," he said, reaching over to place the box on the rocking chair. "I am leaving you something to remember me by."

a

shift

in the weather

❧

1990

In the spring of her junior year at Michigan State, Alice's father called with what was, in her estimation, horrific news. He'd gotten her a summer job in his small Ohio hometown working in a bank. This was the last thing she expected from the man who paid her Visa bills and quietly replenished her account every time she bounced a check. And besides that, she already had plans to teach sailing at Martha's Vineyard with her boyfriend, Mike. They had spent the last two summers together: freshman year working at Meldrum's in Manhattan, and the following year taking intensive Italian on what was essentially an extended booze cruise through the Mediterranean.

It was as if her father, the devoted golfer, had chipped a divot in her life. But no matter how loudly she protested, he would not back down. The Ohio job was not a punishment, he insisted. She needed to focus on her career. Working in a bank would open her eyes. She would be staying with Grandpa Bill until August.

Alice's job was the butt of a lot of jokes at school that spring.

"If you're summering in Newburg, Ohio, look Ollie up," Mike told a large group of friends gathered at The Peanut Barrel. "She'll be doling out dineros at the People's Bank on Main Street."

Alice, laughing, took a mock bow.

Driving her Volkswagen Gulf on I-90 after a brief visit home to take care of all of her gynecological, opthomological, and dental checkups, Alice tried to think positively. It felt a little like fitting the small lip of a balloon onto a helium tank.

I will only be here six weeks. Lake Erie is beautiful. I will diet and read a lot. I will spend every weekend sunning on the beach. She lit a Marlboro Light as the Talking Heads played on the radio, and decided the distance would only enhance her relationship with Mike. The summer might lack excitement, but it would provide her with an excellent chance to detox and reflect.

Late that afternoon, she turned off the highway, passing the placard on the outskirts of town that read:

NEWBURG
Easternmost track of the Western Reserve.
Settled 1800.

Main Street still looked exactly like the nineteenth-century postcards that hung in burnished gold frames in the post office. The same gazebo dominated the town square. The bank was now a tearoom, the old inn a funeral parlor, and the five-and-dime had become a diner, but all of the brick facades remained unchanged. The funeral-parlor windowpanes still sported hearts and initials etched by newlyweds in the late 1800s when the building was the Rosemont Inn, a destination for honeymooners.

It's quaint, she thought as she turned down Lakeview by the Book Barn, but Mike, the snob, would hate it: no Third Edition, no Belle Haven Yacht Club. He once told her that when he thought about Ohio all he could picture were cornfields and Dairy Queen poster children.

His attitude was not so different from her parents, who kept their distance as well. Her father was raised on Russell Street, in a house that was now the Depot Inn, home to Marge's famous lasagna. After Georgetown University he'd returned to Ohio only briefly to work at Lake County National Bank before moving to Michigan and starting up the tool-and-die company in Detroit. Alice's mother didn't like Michigan any better than she'd liked Ohio and fled the Midwest every chance she got, which was a lot. They were always too geared up—fundraisers, tennis, traveling—to give Ohio more than a pass through. Like migratory birds pausing midflight, they only touched down once or twice a year.

For his part, Alice's grandfather, Bill, wanted little to do with his son, Gerard, and his "cha-cha" wife, Michelle. Even though Bill was no Ohio bumpkin—he'd traveled to Mongolia and canoed around the Seychelles—he couldn't stand to hear Michelle prattle on about celebrities she'd run into on the Med, or the charity event she was chairing to benefit sick children she'd never laid eyes on, or the tennis championship she'd won thanks to Dan, the pro, and his grueling workouts. Sometimes in the middle of one of her spiels, he'd get up midsentence, take Alice's hand, and walk down to the beach or out onto the deck overlooking Lake Erie to watch the sunset.

When Alice arrived, Carmela, Bill's housekeeper, met her at the door.

"Just in time for cocktails," she said, gesturing toward the room beyond where a group of octogenarians were gathered around two bridge tables.

"It's a good thing you arrived when you did. An hour from now he might not have recognized you." Carmela had to reach up to give Alice a hug. Then she picked up her bag and led her into a living room, jammed full of masks, knives, miniature wooden tribal people, and elaborately carved ebony walking sticks, vestiges of Bill's adventurous past.

This summer she'd actually have a chance to check out his collection. She applauded herself for her persistent upbeat mindset. Carmela dropped the bag by the stairs and they continued on toward the bridge tables. It seemed to take all that time for Bill to figure out who was coming toward them.

Finally, when she was standing before him he sprang up from his seat. "It's Alice!" he shouted. "How're you doing, kiddo?" He gave her a couple of sound thwacks on the back.

Every year Alice braced herself for signs of decline, but every year his hair, curly and gray with a swath of skunk white at the temples, remained the same. His arms were still sinewy, his grip strong. The only concession to age was the colostomy bag, which sloshed a little when he squeezed her.

Bill looked back toward the table. Did she know Mrs. Kimble? Her son, Don, was the owner of Waverly Used Cars on Main. The

other man was Stan Olner, his oldest friend, the man who'd purport-
edly invented the pop top. "And you know Marcy," he said. Alice
nodded. Marcy, a small Italian woman, had recently retired from
Newburg High School, where she had been the principal for thirty-
seven years. She had been Bill's constant companion since Peggy, his
wife, had died more than twenty years before.

"We're going to have a great summer!" Bill said, sitting back
down at the table. Behind him the angry lake roiled outside the
picture window. "Go on upstairs and unpack."

The next morning Alice woke up at six. She didn't have to
be at the bank until nine, but she was hot and agitated and her
stomach hurt. The more she tossed and turned the more obvious
it became that sleep was a futile pursuit. *This must be what hap-
pens*, she decided, *when a person goes to bed at eight.*

She had gone upstairs to unpack the night before, and by
the time she came down, Bill had announced that it was 5:00
p.m. and the bar was open. Carmela appeared with a tray filled
with four triple Manhattans in oversize copper goblets. Alice
pulled a chair up behind him. Bridge was a mystifying game
and no one seemed inclined to explain the rules once they
started. She ended up in the kitchen, helping Carmela with
the pastrami sandwiches and polishing off a large bag of Lay's
sour-cream-and-onion potato chips, which was probably why
she'd spent most of the night feeling like she was going to
puke.

By eight, they were all shuffling out the door. When Alice
went up to her room the clock by the bed read 8:14. She sat down
and stared at the pink paisley wallpaper on the opposite wall. Bill
walked by on the way to his room.

"Is your clock set?" He swayed back and forth in the doorway. "I don't want you to miss work. I never really get going until ten these days."

Alice nodded.

When he closed the door, she fell back on her pillow. "What am I going to do all summer?" she whispered. Her voice sounded tinny, like a child's.

Ben Broder, the trust manager, met her in the lobby at nine. He led her upstairs to the third floor to a cubicle near the back of a long, narrow room with pumpkin-colored walls. To her right, a large woman with a half-eaten apple on her desk was speaking urgently into her phone. She smiled bleakly at Alice and then turned away to continue her conversation. On Alice's desk someone had placed a large stack of papers.

"You just have to check the numbers," Ben explained, leaning over the desk. He looked like the type of person (yellowing buckteeth, polyester button-down) who might smell, so Alice scooched her chair back.

"Punch them into the ad machine and make sure they stack up. Sometimes they move too fast downstairs and make a mistake." Alice nodded. If everything was OK, she could put the papers in the out-box. If not, she should bring the problem to him. He looked at her to see if this made sense, absentmindedly tapping his pencil on the top of the partition. She couldn't believe this was her job.

Why would her father put her up to this when she had barely passed Algebra I in high school? She wasn't enrolled in business school. Didn't he know that? Her brother Ray was the financial wizard; everyone knew Alice was not inclined that way. Was the job payback for all her parties? Her frivolous spending? Did he even care about her or any of her goals? What the hell was he thinking?

"OK," she said. "Is there anything else?"

"Oh, no!" Ben gave her a big toothy grin. "If you can do this for us, you have no idea what a big help you'll be. We got these new-fangled computers in the conference room but no one knows how to work them yet."

The woman with the apple hung up the phone and turned toward them.

She was middle-aged—Alice guessed forty—with pressed, wavy hair that reminded Alice of a hairdo she'd seen in her history of film class: Katherine Hepburn in the one with the leopard. She wore a black-and-white polka-dot dress with a thin, black patent-leather belt riding up under her voluminous breasts. A large mole was wedged into the crease on the side of her nose.

"This is Linda Strickner," Ben said, putting a hand on her shoulder. "She's been with us for twenty-two years. Can you believe that?"

"I can believe it." Linda had the lopsided smile of a stroke victim. She held her hand out to Alice. It was so thick and sticky it felt like homemade Play-Doh.

Ben peeked into two other cubicles, both empty.

"Well, Linda will make sure you meet everyone," he said. "My office is down at the other end of the hall."

He walked away, listing slightly to the left. Linda picked up her apple and leaned back in her chair.

"So, you home on vacation?" Linda bit into the apple. Juice spurted out onto her dress.

"Yeah, my dad got me the job, but I'm not really from here. I'm staying with my grandfather this summer."

"Bummer," Linda said. "Unless you want to do this for a living?"

"I'm not sure what I want to do. I guess my dad thinks I should figure it out."

Linda threw the apple core into her wastebasket. "That makes sense. Let me know if you need help with anything."

The question that plagued Alice while she worked was whether she and Mike would last the summer. Lately he was drinking and getting high all the time, and it didn't seem like he cared about her one way or the other. When he was drunk he was completely out of control. At the Deke summer send-off in May a freshman named Patty had used the crowded couch as an excuse to plop down on his lap. Alice had forgotten her sweater, and when she returned for it, she caught Patty flinging her arm around his neck. Last fall the captain of the women's swim team yanked him down from the Halloween hayride and kissed him on the back lawn by the senior quad. Her close friend, Missy, witnessed that one. It had often felt like a full-time job fending off women, and the effort made her feel old and haggard. Mike was adept at deflecting the blame.

"I didn't sit on her lap!" he'd say. Or, "She kissed me! I was so drunk I barely remember it."

On the phone last night, Alice had asked Missy whether she thought he would hook up with someone else over the summer, and she'd said, "Well, if he does, it'll just be a fling."

"Girls are probably swarming all over him on Martha's Vineyard," Alice said.

"So, who cares? You're no wallflower. He's lucky to have you, that schmuck. Go out yourself, and fling, fling, fling."

But Missy didn't know what she was talking about. She'd never been to Newburg.

Around eleven thirty, Linda got up and invited Alice to lunch at Arby's. They stopped at a cubicle down the hall to pick up a woman named Harriet who was as thin and lanky as Olive Oyl. She had a large mass of brown hair that swirled up like chocolate pudding into a peak. She might have been a little older than Linda, but it was hard to tell for sure; an enormous pair of gold, wide-rimmed glasses obscured most of her face. On the walk over to Arby's she went on and on about her cat, Brody. At the table, she unwrapped her ham-and-cheese sandwich, smoothed the edges of the tinfoil with her knobby hands, and pressed her white paper napkin into her lap. She stopped talking and bowed her head.

"She always says grace," Linda whispered to Alice.

Linda had ordered two Arby's Double-R Bar sandwiches, curly fries, a Jamocha milk shake, and a huge Coke. The more she purchased, the queasier Alice felt. By the time she reached the counter, the only thing she could stomach was the side salad.

"He was up all night yowling." Harriet finished her prayer and made the sign of the cross. "And you know I'm already dealing with Max."

"Tell Alice about Max," Linda said, squirting horseradish on her sandwich.

Harriet wiped her mouth daintily with the napkin. "I have four cats," she said, counting out on her fingers as if she was talking to a child. "Brody, Max, Malcolm, and Steve."

"They're all named after her ex-boyfriends," Linda interjected, her mouth full of food.

"No!" Alice laughed.

"Linda, you are the worst," Harriet shook her head. "Anyway, Max is getting old and he can't find the litter box, so I don't get much sleep these days."

"Do you know what she does?" Linda turned to Alice, her mouth full. "She's covered her entire bedroom with newspaper and every time that cat pees, she cleans it up."

"All night long?" Alice looked at Harriet. "How many times a night does he go?"

"Three or four," Harriet said. "I'm used to it, although I do get tired in the afternoon. Sometimes I just want to put my head down on the desk."

"Have you ever heard of anything crazier?" Linda laughed. "All for a cat!"

"To you he's just a cat!" Harriet, obviously used to the razzing, shook her tiny fist at Linda. Turning to Alice, she said, "Do you have any pets?"

"We had a dog named Shane," Alice said. "She used to pee on our oriental rugs too before the vet put her to sleep."

"That's too bad," Linda said.

"Yeah, all that pee didn't go over too well with my mom."

On Friday, driving home from work, Alice lit one cigarette after another, her hands shaking. She felt marooned. It seemed like all of her friends had been teleported to more enviable locales where the guys were gorgeous and it was always dollar-beer night. The long weekend gaped like an open wound. She stopped at the Book Barn on the way home, looking for a romance novel. The shopkeeper, a middle-aged man with a mullet, only had two Danielle Steeles left and Alice had read them both.

Before dinner she decided to call Mike. Carmela was making fried catfish and the smell in the kitchen drove Alice out of the room before she could even offer assistance with the meal. She hadn't heard a word from him since he'd arrived on the Vineyard the week before. He was staying with his uncle Rob and aunt Krissie and their four kids, who were all in college or graduate school. She dialed the number he had scrawled on a napkin. After the fourth ring, someone picked up, burped loudly, then hung up. She dialed the number again. "What?" yelled the boy on the other end. Alice put the phone down. If she had been there, she would have been laughing in the background, the way she laughed when Mike and his friends swallowed goldfish or blew beer out of a bong. From this distance, though, it didn't seem funny at all.

After she hung up, she headed downstairs, where she found Bill and Marcy on the couch, singing along with a phone commercial: "Reach out, reach out and touch someone!"

When they saw that Alice was watching they really hammed it up, swaying and clapping along.

"Nice, guys." Alice laughed.

"We don't need much entertainment," Marcy said, playfully yanking on Bill's ear.

When Dan Rather came back on, Marcy leaned back over her solitaire game and Bill picked through the pistachio bowl in his lap. Alice plopped down in the chair next to them.

"So how is the Dustman?" Bill said.

"We don't call him that anymore," Alice said. "He stopped answering to that name when we went to college." He had in fact literally stopped answering to the name, probably because the story behind it was too embarrassing to carry with him past graduation.

Bill held out the pistachios. Alice shook her head. "Does he have your number here?"

"I can't reach him," Alice said. "He's out on Martha's Vineyard."

"Is he coming to visit?" Marcy asked, one card midair.

"I seriously doubt it."

"Well, why in the world not?" Bill said.

Alice didn't want to say that Ohio wasn't exactly a destination. "He's having the time of his life."

"Oh, you'll see," Marcy said. "Pretty soon he'll realize how much he misses you. If he doesn't, phooey on him."

"Hey, I have an idea," Bill said, popping a pistachio into his mouth. "Do you want to see my statues?"

Alice and Bill moved to the living room. "African people come up with supernatural explanations for everything. For instance," he said, picking up a small statue of a woman with a pocket book and high heels, who had her hair coiled up in an elaborate, snake-like bun, "this is my otherworld spirit lover. A diviner on the Ivory Coast went into a trance and told me he had met her and this is what she looked like." He handed the statue to Alice.

"This was back when Peggy, your grandmother, was alive. He said I should spend at least one night a week with my spirit lover or she would get mad and wreak havoc on my house. Of course, it's all rubbish, but when Peggy got sick a couple of months later, I did kind of creep around this old gal. Once or twice I even slept with her under my pillow, hoping for some divine intervention."

He walked to the other side of the mantle and plucked another statue.

"Nigerian people believe that older women are the owners of the world. This is a fertility statue." He held it up for Alice to see: a short, squat woman with a face like a walnut, eyes like saucers, and breasts that hung so low she looked like a potbellied man. "See how her breasts are slack. This is a life giver, a woman who has suckled many babies. The man who sold it to me thought she was the most beautiful thing in his store."

Alice blushed. He put the statue down and moved around the room, pulling out walking sticks and masks and statues. Finally, he came to a tiny, bandy-breasted woman with big, hoop earrings and an elaborate, turquoise dress.

"This is a Nigerian Takindi," he said. "She has the power to cure people. You owe her a sacrifice, a goat or some millet, if she fixes you."

Alice turned the Takindi over and over in her hands. She closed her eyes and made a wish for peace of mind, for happiness, for an end to the panicky, empty feeling that kept washing over her. When she opened her eyes, Bill was staring at her.

"I was praying," she said.

He took the statue out her hands.

"You didn't do it right," he said. "You go like this." He bent down and positioned the statue by Alice's left leg. Then he closed his eyes and whispered what sounded like "chee, chee, chee" as he traced the outline of her body with the carving.

"There," he said, "you're all better now."

And, as if in answer, the phone rang.

"It's for you, sweetie," Marcy called from the other room.

"Told you." Grandpa Bill winked.

Alice picked up the phone, which Marcy had set down on the card table. She glanced around the room to make sure that none of the adults were hovering before saying hello. The lake outside the window was as still as glass.

"Alice, this is Dr. Rooney. We just finally got hold of your mother's housekeeper. She gave my nurse your number out there."

"I'm sorry, who is this?"

"Dr. Rooney, your gynecologist. I'm afraid your thyroid has gone a little wonky."

On Sunday, Alice's mother called. Over and over again, she asked Alice, "What's new? What's new?" but, as usual, before Alice could tell her about Dr. Rooney or anything else, she launched into a monologue about her tennis partner Sally, her sainted coach Dan, and the size of the mobile phone she'd procured from Alice's father. "It's like hoofing around town with a frozen meatloaf in my bag."

In the late afternoon, Alice played gin rummy with Bill. When they finished, she drove over to the pharmacy and then to Dairy Queen for a brownie sundae. Her stomach was so bloated afterward she decided to skip dinner and take a walk and think about her predicament. On Heather Road, she spotted Linda washing an ancient Pinto in the driveway of a small brick ranch-style house. Linda was singing along with Bob Seger's "Running against the Wind." While she worked she hopped and danced and shook her substantial behind. Alice crossed the street, hoping for a discreet escape route, but Linda turned to dip the sponge into her bucket and caught sight of her.

"Hey," Alice said. "I didn't know you lived here. I'm staying right around the corner."

"I knew that," Linda said. She plodded over to the boom box and turned down the volume. "When you said you were staying with Bill, I knew exactly where you were. Everyone knows Bill."

"Mama! Tewephone!" A large, brown-haired boy of about ten or eleven appeared in the doorway flapping his arms up and down. He was too big to be making such a scene. Clearly there was something wrong with him. His eyes slanted downward and his mouth hung open, revealing enormous buckteeth.

"Who is it?" Linda yelled, but he just flapped his arms harder and jumped up and down, his mouth hanging open, his white undershirt too small for his gelatinous belly. He was wearing fuzzy, banana-shaped slippers.

"Oh, great," Linda said, wiping her hands off on her pants. "That's Philip, by the way."

Alice waved at Philip. He smiled and flapped his arms in her direction.

"Tewephone! Tewephone! Tewephone!" he yelled.

"Well, I won't keep you," Alice said. "See you on Monday."

"Hey, why don't you come in?" Linda picked up the bucket and headed over to a pile of towels on the other side of the car. "My husband just sold his soul for this ginormous projection TV and the game's about to start."

"Well." There had to be a way out, but Alice couldn't come up with it fast enough.

"Come on. I'm making Skyline Chili—you've had Skyline before?"

"Nope," Alice said.

"My husband Don makes the best Skyline Chili. It's got cinnamon in it. You'll think you died and went to Heaven."

The front door opened into the living room, a tiny rectangle with a fuzzy pea-green armchair and a brown plaid couch. A cuckoo clock hung on the wall. They stopped in the kitchen so Linda could take the phone call, but there was no one on the line. Down in the basement, a skinny, bald man sat in front of an enormous TV. Philip had run over to the opposite side of the room and was standing in a play area sectioned off with piles of orange milk crates. Mountains of stuffed animals, a train table, and various Lego creations were scattered around him.

"Hey, come here," he called.

"Wait a minute, Philip, I'm going to introduce Alice to Dad," Linda said.

"Now! Now! Now!" Philip yelled.

What a pain in the ass, Alice thought and headed toward the toys.

"Hey, Don, this is Alice, Bill's granddaughter, the one who's working at the bank."

"Hi, Alice." Don swiveled around in his chair. Alice waved. Don looked tall and gangly enough to have made a great basketball player. There was a Budweiser in the cup holder of his La-Z-Boy and an ashtray on top of a stack of phone books beside it. The basement smelled of smoke and mildew. Philip took hold of her hand and dragged her toward a train set in the middle of his play area.

"You like trains? I got lots of trains. You got a best friend? I got a best friend named Eddy. I always let Eddy play with my trains. See I can play with them when you go home. I can share with you. I know how to do that." He handed her a blue engine.

"Thanks," Alice said.

On Monday she received a postcard from Mike with a picture of the Cape Poge Lighthouse on Chappaquiddick. On the back he had drawn an enormous smiley face and scrawled, "Miss you!" at the bottom.

It was pathetic, Missy agreed when she phoned the next day. "Listen," she said. "Stephanie saw him at a party. She told me that—how'd she put it? I don't want you to freak out, OK? He was drunk as a skunk, and she said, 'He didn't look like a guy who had a girlfriend.'"

"Thanks for telling me. That's just what I need to hear right now." Alice's heart whooshed and then fluttered. She struggled for breath. Perhaps it was psychosomatic; Dr. Rooney had mentioned a sluggish heartbeat was a symptom.

"What? I'm telling you for your own good. Go out and have some fun. Screw that no-good schmuck!"

The next night Mike called. Alice was lying on the deck reading *People* magazine.

"How's my Buckeye?" he said.

"Fine."

"I'm sorry I haven't called. It's just crazy out here. I have to be at work at seven, and then every night the guys are like, 'Let's hit The Crab Shack,' and I'm like, 'Guys, I can't take it anymore. I'm going to fuckin' die!' But then we do it again. So even though I'm dying to call you, I never get a chance."

"Well, it sounds like you're having fun," she said. A large rainbow-colored sailboat glided by on the lake.

"How about you, Ollie? Have you embezzled any funds? Maybe you should so you can buy a ticket to come see me."

"Ha, ha. My dad thinks I should learn how to save money, remember?"

"Maybe I could buy you a ticket."

"Or you could come here."

"And do what?" He laughed. "Stare at the corn?"

"Maybe. Listen, I've got to run, there's someone at the door for me." That line had been Missy's suggestion.

"If you're not going to dump him," she said. "At least make him think you're up to something."

Every day Alice ended up at Arby's with Linda and Harriet mainly because she lacked an alternative plan. Linda turned out to be a maniacal sports fan. She filled their lunch hours with play-by-play analyses of Indians games, which didn't seem to bore Harriet at all. The sports fixation was the reason they'd purchased such a large TV. It had cost Don, a truck driver, a month's salary. Harriet also had season tickets to the Indians games. She usually went with members of her church group, a set of middle-aged people, single for various reasons.

Harriet and Linda made no bones about their contempt for Mike when Alice mentioned that she had a pseudo-boyfriend who had no plans to visit her over the summer.

"Just write him off," Harriet said. "Who needs that? I'd rather be alone."

"That's right," Linda said.

"Or focus on school," Harriet said. "I made that mistake once, taking off, marrying a shit."

According to Linda, the shit in question was Greg, who had been gone for years. California, possibly. Harriet had most recently dated a bicyclist named Wolf, but he, too, was long absent. Cats had replaced men, according to Linda, for better or worse.

"What are you studying?" Linda asked Alice, before taking a final pull on her straw and finishing off her shake with a loud gurgle.

"That's a tough one," Alice said. For the most part her focus had been on partying and hanging out with Mike. Before she'd settled on the journalism major, she'd wanted to major in psychology, mostly to figure out what made her parents tick. Sophomore year she'd tried philosophy, but 101 was a joke. Mr. Dreiser, a Jesus look-alike, often sounded more like the Grim Reaper than a teacher.

"You think you're in the prime of your lives, but you are decaying," he would say, brandishing his pointer. "Your cells are now beginning that slow death march that will bring you low sooner than you can even imagine."

"I'm a journalism major," Alice said. "There's no money in it. My parents were shocked, but my brother Ray thought I'd be good at it."

"I wanted to be an English professor," Linda said. "But—" She stopped and bit into her sandwich.

"I didn't know that. What happened?" Harriet said.

"I went to my career counselor or guidance counselor or whatever you call them, and said that I wanted to go to college. I knew my parents couldn't afford it, but I had straight As. I asked her how I could get a scholarship."

"What'd she say?" Alice said.

"She said, 'Funny, you just don't look like a scholar.'"

"Yikes," Harriet said.

Linda laughed. "I should have said, 'Funny, you don't look like a bitch.' But I didn't. I was too young. I just left."

On Friday night Don, Philip, and Alice were in the basement eating popcorn when Don pulled Alice aside and asked whether she would watch Philip on July 8. It was their fifteenth anniversary and he wanted to take Linda to Luigi's on the lake.

"Fifteen years! That's great. How'd you two meet?"

The game came back on. Don rotated toward the TV.

"Blind date," he said. "I always tell people I met Linda on a blind date and have been blind ever since."

On the Fourth of July, Harriet invited Alice to her block party. Harriet lived in a tiny bungalow on a street about ten blocks from the lake. Most of the guests were small children, who spent the entire party screaming and running through sprinklers while devouring red-white-and-blue popsicles.

After hot dogs and pop, Harriet took Alice, Linda, and Philip in to see the cats and escape the relentless high-pitched shrieking. She had positioned a baby gate in front of her bedroom door so that Max, the incontinent cat, couldn't escape. Alice was overcome with the hot, agitated feeling she had every time she'd visited her grandmother in the nursing home. Max was spinning around in the middle of the room. Harriet said he was chasing his tail, which was probably mystifying to him as he was almost blind. Around and around he went like a small planet rotating.

The next day Mike called, saying that he had bought her a ticket to come see him that Friday.

"I'm sorry," Alice said. "I already have plans."

"With who?"

"Philip."

On the day before the anniversary celebration, Linda, Harriet, and Alice went to Arby's. Linda pulled out a yellow legal pad on which she had written the babysitting instructions.

"One dessert, no matter how much he begs. You have to really help him brush his teeth. He'll just run the toothbrush over his tongue and spit, unless you watch him. He *has* to pee before bed or he'll wet the bed. Nothing but Dr. Seuss or he has nightmares. Routine is very important, so I've numbered everything. I don't mean to be weird about it, but he'll freak if you don't follow the schedule . . ."

Alice took the legal pad and looked it over.

"Also, his medication. You don't need to give it to him unless he starts to wheeze or seems to have trouble breathing."

"Asthma?"

"Congestive heart failure, actually."

Alice stared at the napkin holder on the table. Linda was trying to rip open her Double-R Bar sauce and didn't look up.

"He doesn't really have it . . . well, he has it on and off. The doctor says he'll be fine as long as we keep his diet in check. Lots of Down's kids have it."

"Oh," Alice said. She glanced through the instructions again. "Do you write this all out every time you have a babysitter?" she asked.

"We've never had a babysitter before." Linda took a sip of her milkshake.

"Never?"

"Oh, my mom—when she was alive, but since then, no," Linda said. "We kind of like staying home."

Alice was flabbergasted. She'd had babysitters in all shapes and colors, a long, motley parade. She'd had nicknames for all of them: the Power Mower, Hairy Nostrils, the Mashed Potato, Hitler, Big Betty.

Harriet cleared her throat. "I know this is off the subject, but if you guys have extra newspapers, would you mind bringing them in? I'm running low."

"Gosh, Harriet," Linda said. "I'm going to do you a favor one day and smother those cats."

When Alice showed up for babysitting the next night, Linda looked anxious, but Don dragged her out the door saying they'd be home around midnight. Philip led Alice down to play with his trains. Later, while they were eating Linda's chili, he told her about his week at school and the developmental-disabilities program at the YMCA.

"So then Eddy decides he's a steam roller and he gets down on the floor and he starts going like this." Philip got down on the floor to demonstrate. "And he goes vroom, vroom, vroom, right into Mr. Sanders. Boy, was he mad. Then he tried to pick Eddy up by his ear, but Eddy kept going vroom, vroom, vroom right into the salad cart and all the salad fell down!"

"Oh, no," Alice laughed.

"It was the best day. No yucky salad!" Philip clapped and then flapped his arms.

Over dinner, Philip pelted Alice with questions while downing a chili dog and dripping sauce all over the floor.

"You got a best friend?" he said.

"Yes, his name's Mike."

"You guys like trains?"

"Well . . ."

"You got a mom?"

"Yes."

"You got brother?"

"Yup."

"You got sister?"

Alice hesitated. "Used to."

"Used to?"

"She's in Heaven."

"That's good. She's lucky."

"Really?"

He nodded. "You got a mom? She's got a name for you?"

"She named me Alice."

"Yeah. My mom's got the Phil Buster, the Phil Pill, Phil the Grill, and she's got a song goes like . . ." And here he went into a long insensible song that Alice couldn't follow, though she tried to look interested.

"You got other friends?" he said.

"Sure," Alice said.

"They play what you want to play?"

"Sometimes."

"No broccoli," he added, pushing away his plate.

"Not even for a Dum-Dum?"

"OK." He reached for the plate just like Linda said he would.

The bedtime routine was exhausting. Philip smeared toothpaste all over the bathroom, and tried to wipe some off in her hair. His prayer went on for ten minutes and seemed to include everyone in the neighborhood. While she read *Oh, the Places You'll Go!* he bounced on the bed:

"You have brains in your poop!

You have feet in your poop!

You can steer your poop

Any direction you poop!"

When Alice finally got him into bed and leaned down to kiss him good night, he threw his arms around her neck, giving her a hug that was more forceful than any she'd ever received.

"I'll play what you want next time you come," he said. "You can bring your toys."

After Philip was asleep, Alice slipped back into his room. She pulled the African Takindi out of her pocket and shook it over his heart.

"Chee, chee, chee," she whispered.

On Saturday night, Alice's mother called again.

She didn't bother with hello.

"Did Dr. Rooney reach you?" she whispered. Alice could hear the TV blaring in the background.

"Yes," Alice said. "I spoke to him."

"What in the world . . . well, oh my God, I'm sorry. I can't even get it out. What in the world . . . I know that's not good . . . a call like that . . . what did he want? You know they wouldn't tell me? They wouldn't tell your own mother . . . I mean twenty . . . they should *still* tell the mother . . . Oh my God, I don't even want to know . . ."

Alice waited. Many things were happening outside the window on the water. She could barely hear her mother's voice through the phone. It was as if a fault had opened up in the earth and her mother had fallen in, to remain wedged in that tight space in the ground forever.

Finally, her mother stopped babbling.

"I'm a little hyperthyroid," Alice said.

"Holy Mother of Christ! Holy . . . phew, OK then! You can't imagine what I was . . ."

"He called in the prescription. I've been taking it for a couple of weeks and I feel pretty good. I'll go for more tests when I get home."

"You? Oh, well, well. Thank God that's all it is! He wouldn't even tell me! You know you never know these da . . . Mary Jenkins's daughter . . . I know—"

"I'm not pregnant, mom."

"No, you're too smart for that. I'm glad that's taken care of. I'm coming out soon, by the way. I've got the Rain brothers here painting the house. It took me six months to get them so I have to do that first and then I'll figure out a time to visit if I can."

After she hung up, Alice went down to the deck, sat in a lawn chair, and watched the water, which had gone from crystalline to gray and fitful while she was speaking with her mother. The thing about Lake Erie was that a storm could come up out of nowhere at a moment's notice. According to Grandpa Bill, boaters had to be very cautious, always on the lookout for a shift in the weather. Alice was reminded of her philosophy professor and his dire predictions. The sun was going down behind a cloud, the only sign a pink glow that permeated the edges. When she was older, there would be real problems. Who would help her through them? There had to have been a phone call when the doctor told Linda about Philip's prognosis or when Harriet's husband beat her for the first time or when Grandma Peggy died. Reach out and touch someone. The phone commercial made it seem so easy.

Mike started phoning incessantly, jealous of the mysterious "Philip guy." But Alice, reading in the chaise lounge or disrupted in the middle of gin rummy, had started to wonder why she wanted him so badly. The conversations were inane: So and so was drunk and fell off the boat. So and so got hit by a car, but was so drunk he bounced like a ball when he hit the pavement. Meanwhile, when Alice told him about Linda and Don or Harriet and the cats, he laughed, as if Alice were describing sitcom characters, people too outrageous to be believed.

One day early in August, right before she returned to school, Alice told Mike she was going over to Lakeland Community College to pick up a course catalog for Linda. Maybe that would inspire her to return to school.

"She'd make a great teacher," Alice said.

"Is she the one with the cats or the retard?" Mike said.

From then on whenever he called Alice said she had to go, even when the only thing pressing was a trip to Dairy Queen. One day, sounding desperate, he announced that he was sending her another plane ticket.

"I don't know." Alice was sitting next to Bill, who had dozed off with a bowl of pistachios in his lap. She reached over and put them on the table.

"I don't think I can," she said. "I've got a lot going on this weekend."

"Really?" Mike said. "Like what?"

A sound like gushing water filled the room. Bill's colostomy bag was filling up.

"You'd be surprised," Alice said.

trees

from

heaven

2003

The funeral had already been held. Sean said he was sorry he hadn't contacted her—he hadn't been thinking clearly. Alice said it was OK even though a ringing had started up, insistent as a schoolyard bell, in her ears. It was all she could do to mumble good-bye. After she hung up she could not get up from the chair. The bird clock on the wall struck 11:00 a.m., and the northern cardinal chirruped, "What? What? What?" Alice stared at the phone. It wasn't until it rang again, startling her, that she picked up her keys and walked out of the house. If her husband Ed had called at that moment, she could have told him where she was going, but she could not have explained why.

The radio station where Alice had worked with Sean seven years before was on Bishop. From what he had told her in e-mails over the years, it wasn't housed in the dilapidated old building with the asbestos floor tiles and the rusted-out toilets anymore. Now it was in a new building two streets away. The newsroom actually had windows.

Alice had worked at the station for three years before her children were born and ever since had reminisced about those fleeting moments of independence and productivity. Back then she thought herself a fearless journalist. She had traveled into the ghetto and been told by a young man in baggy jeans and a Run-DMC T-shirt that she was a fool to stand on the corner with her microphone "looking like target practice." In the succeeding years, she told the same stories about her time at the radio station over and over: the interview with the mayor, the prison tour, David Harmon's impassioned speech on municipal water shortages, and the ineptitude of the school board. People in her later life knew that she had been a radio reporter, but most of them had never heard of her, or they didn't remember hearing her. Her name had been different back then.

When Alice was there, five people worked in the news department. The news director was an aging hippie named Robert Jones, who was good-natured and scatterbrained. Carl Ryer, the business reporter, was a young, ambitious man from Indiana who was almost always too caught up with the automobile industry to interact with his colleagues. The other two reporters were Alice's friends. Sean, a young, soft-spoken black man who had graduated from Michigan State, hoped to take over as news director when Robert retired to San Francisco. Sean reveled in the daily machinations of the newsroom, preferring to allocate the stories rather than cover them. Alice thought he would make a fantastic news director because he actually had a Rolodex, and he always looked interested, even when the stories—one day, the origin of the toilet seat—were inane.

Her other friend at the station was a black woman in her late thirties who had been born Mary Anne Steck and renamed herself Suma Shahid. Alice never learned whether it was a political statement or simply a nom de plume. Suma was the single mother of an eleven-year-old girl named Adla, who often came into the radio station after school and did her homework on the ramshackle black leather sofa in the corner of the room.

Suma, the art critic, was herself an objet d'art. Alice once told Sean that rounding the corner to find Suma in her flowing lemon-brown buba and matching kufi cap, hard at work in her dingy cubicle, was like stumbling across a Matisse in an abandoned warehouse. During morning meetings, she chewed on limewood sticks, which she claimed worked better than her toothbrush. She ate peanut-butter stews, chapattis, and jollof rice, all of which smelled enticing when Alice wasn't pregnant. Suma brought her meals to the office in Tupperware and ate them at her desk. One time when Alice was driving home, she heard Suma deliver a report on a congressman's bid for reelection. At the end she paused briefly and then added, "No matter how long a log stays in the water, it doesn't become a crocodile." Of course she was reprimanded. The next morning, Robert said, "You know better than that." Suma shrugged. Had anyone else done it, they might have been fired. Alice began to think there was something almost mystical about Suma, because she did whatever she wanted and nobody harassed her.

Initially, Suma did not like Alice. It started two weeks into the job when Alice wore her Lilly Pulitzer pink-and-green flowered pants into the office.

"Whoa! Turn down the lights," Robert called from his desk.

Suma shook her head, rattling the beads on her silver-and-gold skullcap. "You look like a bad trip, girl."

Nobody would have dared to make fun of Suma, though, in some of her robes, Alice thought she resembled an oversize parrot.

Suma had covered the art beat that Alice coveted for so long that her cubicle might have doubled as a flea-market booth. It was filled with eccentric abstract paintings, including one that resembled a watermelon sitting on a bus. She had a small sculpture of a woman with her arms outstretched toward the sky labeled, *Homage to the Sun*, which Alice secretly called *Fat Woman Hailing a Cab*.

Every time the Detroit Institute of Arts announced a new exhibit or the newsroom received an art-gallery press release, Alice pounced on it. But inevitably during the morning meeting, Suma would mention that she knew Kwambe Mfabe. They had worked together at the Sunrise Café before he was discovered. She landed every story that way. The only time Alice prevailed was when Adla was sick, and Suma stayed home.

Both Suma and Alice covered local news as well. One time when the president delivered his State of the Union, Suma and Alice were told to gather reactions in the city and suburbs. Sitting in the newsroom listening to the speech,

Alice thought him inspiring, but Suma scoffed as he made an enthusiastic prediction about economic renewal and diminishing unemployment. "The eyes of the wise see right through him," she said.

The animosity persisted until one day when Suma's car died in the parking lot. Alice offered her a ride home. Suma accepted, but kept Alice waiting for half an hour while she talked on the phone with a sculptor. She took her time gathering her long black raincoat and Tupperware.

At the time, Alice drove a rusted-out, light-blue 1979 Chevette, which she nicknamed "the blue bomb" later in life and which Ed insisted they drive instead of the BMW her father wanted to give her. In those days, Ed had felt that it was important to make it on their own financially. Alice had her own reasons for complying.

"Are you sure I'm not going to fall through the floor?" Suma asked.

"Sometimes I think I'm going to put my foot through a hole and get sucked out," Alice said, laughing.

"I knew I should have walked," Suma said, but she was smiling too.

They turned right on Shipley and headed past several boarded-up old Victorian houses. On the left side of the street, Alice noticed an emaciated golden retriever running along the sidewalk.

"Look at that dog," Alice said.

"Oh, they're everywhere." Suma hadn't even glanced in the direction of the dog.

"That dog is going to freeze to death," Alice said.

"When an elephant is being killed no one notices the death of a monkey."

Alice thought about riding back to get the dog, taking it home, giving it food and a bath. Why shouldn't she save it? Then a picture formed in her head of the dog leaping over the backseat, biting her in the neck, scratching her and giving her some strange flesh-eating disease. Who knew where that dog had been? If she remembered, she would call the Humane Society.

While she was still debating, Suma motioned for her to pull over. They were in front of a run-down redbrick house with a slanted porch. In the driveway on a mattress were two men in thick black parkas stretched out on their backs. In front of the house, two trees, similar to the ones in front of the station, were bursting up through the broken sidewalk. Robert called them ghetto palms, but Suma said they were trees from Heaven because they had pushed through the cracks like people who'd been buried alive.

A tall, thick-set black man in a long black leather coat stood on Suma's porch with his arms crossed. Alice glanced up and saw Adla staring out of the big picture window on the second floor. She had two high pigtails in her hair. She waved down at Suma, who did not wave back. Perhaps, Alice thought, she didn't want anyone to know a little girl lived up there.

Suma brushed past the man on the porch, ignoring the people on the mattress. She unlocked the door and went inside. The man followed and Adla disappeared from the window. Alice drove away quickly, and when she had made it a safe distance, she locked her doors.

When Alice had been working at the station for a year, her grandfather Bill—really more of a father than her own—died.

Although her mother had warned her that his heart was failing and he was living on a butterfly's wing, it did not make the end any easier. The call came on a Friday morning before work.

When she returned to the station the following week, she could barely function. Everyone offered their condolences, including Carl, who made a point of swiveling around in his chair to mutter his regrets. She returned to her desk after the meeting and rummaged through the papers that had accumulated. Every movement required a concerted effort. All of the news releases looked ridiculous, insignificant. An ad for the City Center Flower Show reminded her that she could no longer show her grandfather anything, not even a single flower. All she wanted to do was lie down on the black couch and go to sleep forever.

She was staring at the flower-show ad when Suma called out to her, "If you're looking for something, you can cover the Reneke exhibit. It starts tonight." She held up a piece of paper over the piles of books and debris that formed a barrier between their two cubicles.

"Thanks," she said. "I've never heard of Reneke."

"You've seen her work." Suma held up the infamous sculpture. "This is one of her pieces."

"I always thought that looked like a fat woman hailing a cab," Alice said.

Suma burst out laughing. Sean peeked around the corner of his cubicle. Suma never laughed.

"You know what they say, girl?"

"I can't wait to hear."

"An old man sitting on the ground sees something the child misses even if he climbs a tree."

Alice worked at the station for two more years, but she left midway through her first pregnancy, afraid that the decrepit building was unhealthy. The floor tiles were coming up, the bathrooms were old and filthy, and the newsroom had no windows. Carl Ryer became convinced that he was suffering from sick building syndrome and left to work in public relations in Chicago. By the time Alice quit, there were only two buildings still standing on the block. Across the street from the station was an abandoned apartment building with two gargoyles perched over the front door. All the windows were gone. Alice sometimes had the feeling that ghosts, or crack addicts, were monitoring her progress along the sidewalk. It grated on her, leaving her nice home each morning to march through the refuse. She felt terrible about the abandoned houses, the brown fields, and the woman who pissed regularly on the street corner outside the station, but what could she do about it?

Right before she left the station, she and Suma were in the recording studio late on a Tuesday night. Suma said she hated to work late because Adla was leaving in two days to spend the whole summer with her father in New York. Alice asked Suma whether she was going to take a vacation herself.

"Why would I do that?" Suma asked, turning away from the sound desk.

"I don't know. You could rest, relax, go somewhere."

"Where do you think I should go?" Suma said.

Alice thought about all the places she would go: Harbor Springs, Cape Cod, the Bahamas, a canoe trip in the Boundary Waters.

"You know what I want to do?" Suma asked.

"What?"

"I'm going to work the land. I'm going to get a patch of garden out at this old farm I know about and plant a huge vegetable garden."

"Really?"

"You've heard the saying, 'If one does not farm, he does not eat.'"

"Yeah," Alice said, "but now we have grocery stores."

When they were done cleaning up that night and Suma had returned from the newsroom with her straw bag to say good-bye, Alice felt bereft.

"I'm going to miss you," she said.

"You're making the right decision," Suma said.

"I am?" Alice was surprised to hear her say that. She thought Suma would be angry with her for deserting.

"I can sense something good coming out of you."

"You can? Like what?"

"Who knows? Another person's heart is a wilderness."

Suma kept looking at Alice as if she realized something about her that either Alice did not want to reveal or that Alice did not even understand herself.

"I'll do your chart," Suma said, putting down her bag and grabbing a notepad lying on a nearby desk. She wrote down Alice's full name and then numbered each letter. When she was done with her calculations, she pulled out a small red book with a sun on the cover.

"You've done something you regret," Suma said.

That was an understatement. What was she referring to? Gary Smith, the scholarship kid she'd gotten kicked out of school for drug dealing when everyone knew her boyfriend Mike Gallagher was the real dealer? That was the worst thing by far. Or was she talking about Mike later in college? The fact that she hadn't gotten him help for his drug addiction in time to stave off the overdose?

"Ah," Suma said, pointing to another group of numbers. "A single partridge flying through the bush leaves no patch."

"What does that mean?" Alice said.

"Your lesson in life is relationships."

When pressed for more information, Suma just shrugged. "I don't have all the answers," she said.

When Alice's son, John Andrew, was born, she entered another dimension. There was no time to write out a grocery list, much less an article. She was completely overwhelmed and sleep-deprived. Whenever she tried to do anything productive, the baby would wail and Alice felt like putting her fist through the computer. She sought out acquaintances in Gymboree and Kindermusik. She made friends with women whose lives, like hers, revolved around nap time. At the same time, Ed was writing furiously at night and on the weekends and he'd started doing some consulting work for Townley Tool and Die. Alice's father was trying to lure him into the family business. One day, Alice's father said he needed to buy a new house for tax reasons and if they wouldn't mind, he'd like to give it to them. Surprisingly, Ed didn't turn him down. Maybe, he said, we ought to accept our good fortune.

Alice had one overriding feeling during this period. She was lucky, she knew, but she was not satisfied. She felt like someone had pegged her to a wall in a museum and placed a "Soccer Mom" placard beside her. The years passed in a blur of diapers, plastic toys, and periodic tantrums. In the end, Alice spent so much time sequestered in her neighborhood, planting her annuals, perusing home-decorating manuals, strolling up to the Farms Market with her babies, that she could no more imagine herself in the ghetto than she could see herself on the moon. As the years went by she grew more and more wary of the city. Garbage pickup was erratic, the streetlights didn't work, the police were shooting too many people, and several school-board members were caught embezzling. The mayor decided not to run for reelection.

Alice only saw Suma once after she left the station. They had planned to meet for lunch. Suma was working at an organic farm in the mornings. She had asked the station if she could work the afternoon shift, and of course, Suma being Suma, they had complied. By that time, Alice was eight months pregnant with her daughter Denise. She had gained forty pounds, thinking that it was her duty to consume as much as she could hold. Simply getting into the Chevette had become an acrobatic feat. The organic farm was almost an hour away from Alice's house. By the time she reached the farm she had to pee and her left leg was asleep. She drove up and parked near the main building, an old white farmhouse with a wraparound porch, where a gray-haired black man in overalls sat eating an apple. He stared at Alice as she struggled to get out of the car. She had to turn, put both feet on the floorboard, and hoist herself up. The man looked amused as she limped over to him.

"I think she's in the tomatoes," he said, pointing to a tiny white building. It seemed like it was three miles away. Her skin itched, the sun was ruthless. As she neared the shed, Suma suddenly popped up among the green vines. Two women, one dressed in a pink suit and one in red, stood in the shade of a small overhang. They turned to Alice but neither smiled.

Suma was wearing a multicolored head wrap and overalls. At first it seemed like she couldn't place Alice. She put her hand up to block the sun. Finally, she waved.

"Hey, girl! How are you?"

"I'm quite large, actually."

"Was today the day we were supposed to meet for lunch?" Suma walked over to her.

"Yeah."

"Shoot, I forgot." Suma looked over at the two women near the shed.

"Oh, well, that's OK," Alice said.

"Can we do it another day?"

Alice was startled. "Sure, I guess."

"That would be great. I feel terrible."

Suma did not look like she felt terrible. She was acting like she had just bumped into Alice by chance. Alice glanced over at the ladies again before she turned around to walk back to the car. They continued to stare at her unhappily.

Over the next few weeks, Alice went over it in her mind. Why hadn't Suma invited Alice to join their group? Why hadn't the women said hello? Why hadn't Suma acknowledged the effort she'd made driving out to the farm? Was she mad at Alice? Why would she be mad? Did those women dislike white people? Were they laughing at her behind her back? Was she left out because she wasn't a member of the sisterhood?

Though Alice lost touch with Suma completely after the farm incident, she and Sean continued to write a couple of times a year. They ended every e-mail with the assertion that they had to meet for lunch before lunch turned into oatmeal at the St. John Senior Center. In the end, it took them six years to do it.

That day Alice arrived at the Sign of the Dove a couple of minutes early, and when Sean finally walked in she was surprised that he was wearing a suit and his hair was turning gray. They exchanged pictures of the kids, they talked about how the kids were doing, the constant fighting, the early morning wake-up calls. Sean told Alice that his wife had decided to home school.

"Thirty-seven percent of the city schools are going to lose accreditation this year," he said. "Too many kids are failing."

When Sean asked Alice what was new, she told him about her work with Tri-County Care, a charity group that raised money by holding quarterly theme parties.

"That's great," Sean said.

"Every summer we have a Fourth of July celebration. It's fun for the kids. Maybe you guys could come out for it," Alice said, then felt terrible. The ticket prices were steep if you were trying to scrape by on a public-radio salary.

"Maybe," Sean said. "It sounds like fun."

"What's new at the station?" Alice asked, placing a dollop of sour cream on her soup.

"What isn't new?" Sean said. According to him, things had been crazy. Robert had left for San Francisco the previous fall, but the station had hired a woman from Indiana to take his place. Sean had decided to stick with the station anyway. He loved public radio and couldn't imagine doing anything else.

"They're a bunch of idiots," Alice said.

"Anyway, there's still a lot to do," he said. The station was short staffed and they were trying to keep up with the mayoral problems, the police shootings, garbage collection problems, potholes, and drug busts.

"If you want to do some freelancing, you can help us out with the city's three-hundredth anniversary," Sean said.

"I'd love to," Alice said, sounding more enthused than she had planned. She had the feeling that Sean found her volunteer updates pathetic.

Then two years passed without a word from Sean. Alice was hard at work on the Tri-County auction trying to convince people to donate their condominiums and cars and heirloom jewelry. Everyone told her that she was doing a great job, but all of the kudos did nothing to alleviate her malaise. She felt run-down and depressed. She screamed at the children when they played with their food or argued about what clothes to wear in the morning. Sometimes, after she dropped them off at school, she crawled back into bed and stared at the ceiling. One morning, Alice's neighbor Ann dropped by to visit. Ann, a clinical psychologist, bore an uncanny resemblance to Joan Rivers. Despite that, Alice figured if anyone could help her, Ann could.

"It's a phase, Alice," Ann said. They were sitting in Alice's great room drinking coffee and watching Regis and Kathie Lee. "Your kids are in school now and you don't know what to do with yourself. Everybody goes through it."

"Really?" Alice said. "It feels much bigger than that."

"Do you know how many times I've heard that?" Ann laughed. She rummaged through her purse for her cigarettes.

"Take some time out for yourself. Make a plan. If you don't feel better in a month or two, I'll send you to Don Richards and he'll give you something to take the edge off."

Alice took up walking in the mornings. She walked for miles and miles along the tree-lined streets, enjoying the sweet fragrances of the lilacs in the spring. She bought an exercise bike and vowed to read a novel a week. She joined the Bikram yoga class in the basement of the Unitarian church and sweated profusely. Ann told her she ought to look for a part-time job. One day after she'd taken the kids to school, she called Sean.

"I was thinking about going back to work part-time. I wanted to let you know in case anything comes up there."

"Well, we'd love that. Of course, you heard about Suma. That's kind of got us stymied right now."

"No. What happened?"

"Oh, boy. I thought you knew. Well, this is tough . . . It's hard for me to even say it. You remember Adla? She was killed last week . . . murdered, actually."

Alice couldn't speak.

"I know. It's a shock. We're all shocked. We can't believe it."

The phone felt like a boulder. Alice tried to say something, but no sound came out.

"She'd gone up to the corner store for some potato chips, and she met up with her neighbor Derek on the way home. They were walking together, when some guy gunned Derek down. Apparently, he was the target. He had dissed the guy's girlfriend, but Adla was standing next to him, so . . ."

"Oh my God."

"The worst part is, I think Suma saw it. Martin saw. I think the whole neighborhood saw. It was really unbelievable. Broad daylight."

"Who's Martin?"

"Suma's brother. He lived with them. It happened last Thursday. We had a memorial on the radio Monday night, but all the newspaper had was a little blurb on page five. I'm not surprised you missed it. Page five. Woman gunned down in broad daylight and it's page-five news. Suma's a mess. She hasn't left the house since the service."

On the way to Suma's to offer her condolences, Alice's car went through a pothole the size of an icefall. She struggled to regain control of the wheel as she passed the seven-cylinder incinerator that blew refuse at the suburbs and had been the subject of much controversy lately. A local environmental group was researching the possibility of a cancer cluster in Alice's suburb due to all the pollution blowing in from the city. Around the next turn, the city rose up in front of her.

From here, she thought, it actually looked like a destination.

Trash lined the street as she exited onto Bishop. It was almost festive, all of the vibrant packages clumped together along the gutter like ribbon unraveling. Where the old Hudson's Department Store used to be, was just a vast expanse of sky. The store had closed five years before, and was demolished the following summer. Alice remembered the day clearly. That morning, Ed had called to her from the driveway. A thin layer of red dust covered his car.

"Can you believe it?" He traced a smiley face on the hood. "We've got dust all the way out here."

Alice drove to the building where they had once worked. It was boarded up. She turned around in the parking lot and headed toward Suma's house. The old apartment building with the gargoyles was gone. In the place of several other buildings were long stretches of prairie grass. She went past the Golden Dragon, the Nail Shack, a nightclub called the Voodoo Lounge. There were no dogs around.

It was not until Alice was sitting in front of Suma's house that she questioned herself. She hadn't spoken to Suma in years. There was not a soul on the street. Alice was parked next to an abandoned house, the windows and doors boarded up and "Keep Out" scrawled in red spray paint across every available surface. In the front yard, a metal trash can smoked. Two wooden chairs with peeling green paint and an old Barcalounger were arranged around the can. Adla had been killed here not two weeks before. Alice looked at the sidewalk, picturing the little girl with the butterfly pigtails lying in a pool of blood.

A beat-up, brown Impala rolled slowly past. Alice hunkered down in her seat. She peeked out the window. Stroh's beer cans littered the sidewalk. A large orange-and-white Nike running shoe hung from a wrought iron fence. A black ski glove dangled from the antennae of the pale-blue Pinto across the street. Suma's next-door neighbor's yard was obscured by a four-foot mountain of filthy plastic children's toys.

She decided she would drop Suma a note. After all, it wasn't right to show up on somebody's doorstep unannounced. As she turned the car around in a driveway, a terrific crunching noise came from under the car. She had backed over a pile of debris.

She pulled forward, stopped, and turned for one last look at Suma's house.

Suma was standing in the picture window in a hunter-green bathrobe, her cornrows pulled back in a ponytail. She did not look anything like her usual self. Later Alice decided it was like seeing an actor backstage without makeup and costume. She stopped the car in the middle of the street, got out, and waved. Suma put her right hand up to the window and pressed her palm against the glass. Alice's legs wobbled. Suma put her palm up against the side of her head and closed her eyes, mimicking sleep, and from this Alice gathered that she was not going to come downstairs, she was going to sleep. Alice nodded. Suma kissed her fingertips and touched the glass. Then she turned and disappeared from view.

opportunity

cost

ও

2006

My name is David Clarke. For the last two decades I have been a high-school economics and sociology teacher in an affluent suburb outside Detroit—a suburb that has had to work hard to maintain its tenuous air of allure. It is situated along the shores of an idyllic lake and boasts several country clubs, two small shopping "villages," and some innocuous architecture— the homes mostly Tudors and Colonials—making it, in short, a pleasant place to reside.

During the sixties and afterward the city became a volatile territory and relations between the city and the suburbs were strained. My wife, Monica, a treasurer in the local chapter of the Jewish Historical Society and the manager of the Defenders Food Bank, fervently believes that we suburbanites abandoned the city, took our businesses and our money, and turned our backs on city dwellers, impoverishing the area and embittering everyone to boot. Of course, many people disagree with her viewpoint. Nevertheless, I think she is correct in surmising that this legacy will be hard to overcome.

An economics teacher, I believe many variables contributed to the rapid deterioration of this Midwestern region, including but not limited to the death of manufacturing, the inability to efficiently and cost-effectively transfer goods from one location to another, and the extreme—I can hear Monica's outrage from here!—demands of the unions. Add to that environmental and government regulations and cheap labor abroad, and the offshoot is the dive we're in.

Introduction to Economics is a terminal class at the high-school level, meant to give students a taste of the discipline. My class is always full because it's an alternative to calculus and many of my students, the sons and daughters of affluent parents, find the practical aspects of the handling, acquisition, and dispersal of money fascinating.

This year we had more girls than boys for the first time in a long time. I also noted that we had two African American students in the class, a girl and a boy. The suburb has slowly become more integrated over the last twenty years, but I would say that even so, less than 5 percent of the student body is black.

On the first day of school, the young man wore khaki pants that had been meticulously ironed if not dry-cleaned, a button-down blue-and-white pin-striped shirt, and loafers with no socks. I noticed his attire because most of the boys at our school wear blue jeans, and the remaining minority favor khakis or cargo pants, most of which are so wrinkled one wonders if they've ever been laundered. Almost all of my students wear tennis shoes, so his gleaming penny loafers were as unusual as the briefcase of dark, polished leather he carried.

Everyone filed into the classroom and sat down. On the first day, most students, if given the option, will gravitate to the back of the class. The boy with the pressed khakis was the second person in the room on the first day of school, but instead of putting as much distance between us as possible, he walked straight toward me, held out his hand, and said, "Good morning. My name is Creighton LaMott."

I greeted him and he took the seat right in front of my desk. He opened his briefcase and extracted a metallic-looking clipboard and a ballpoint pen, which he placed on the desk in front of him.

I gave my introductory spiel replete with my perennial economics trivia quiz: What was the average amount of money left per visit by the tooth fairy in 1950? (Twenty-five cents.) Who was the first African American to have his portrait engraved on a U.S. coin? (Booker T. Washington.) What American company introduced sliced bread? (The Chillicothe Baking Company of Chillicothe, Missouri.) It's a good ice-breaker and the kids always get a kick out of the questions.

Nothing happened that drew my attention to Creighton until a couple of days later when I posited this question: "Does anyone know what 'there is no such thing as a free lunch' means?"

Creighton, who had been doodling, looked up and raised his hand. "Opportunity cost. If one group gets something for free, then another group ends up paying for it."

"That's correct," I said, smiling. I was surprised that someone had actually read ahead in the text to the section on opportunity cost, which states essentially that to get something you must give up something else. There's always a trade-off, in other words.

"I have heard this is a big problem with the niggers," Creighton said.

I wasn't sure I'd heard him correctly. His face was blank; he hadn't said it with any emotion whatsoever, but in the same tone of voice one might say, "The Tigers lost last night." Looking out at the class was like looking at a still frame. Heat surged up into my face.

"Excuse me?" I said.

"Niggers," Creighton said. "You know, lowlifes. They have babies when they're like twelve and then they ride the system. You know what I'm talking about. You know who ends up paying for it."

"I would never have used that term," I said.

Creighton shrugged.

I looked out at the rest of the class. One of the football players, Max Meyer, was snickering in the back row. The African American girl, Sonya Wright, seemed to be holding her breath, her eyes protruding. A girl named Tina Stewart, the newly elected student-body president and head cheerleader, chewed her gum rhythmically with a glazed expression, as if this was all unfolding on television and merited no reaction.

"I won't have any derogatory language in this class," I said. "Do you understand me?"

"Sure," Creighton said, without looking up from his doodling.

That night, when I told Monica what Creighton had said, she looked decidedly nonplussed. "He's differentiating. He's not like them and he wants you to know it."

"Not like who?" I said.

"Niggers," she said.

"I never in my life thought I'd hear you use that word."

"It's no different than saying white trash," she said, but she smiled so I knew she was goading me. Sometimes she thinks it's fun to try to elicit a reaction.

Monica and I met shortly after graduation when I was working at Pierson Elementary right next to the Defender's Food Bank. We were both very fond of Maurice's, the corner deli, and we always seemed to be getting our sandwiches at the same time. Being rather slow on the uptake, it took me six months to ask her out on a proper date, twelve months to propose, and another two years to convince her to move with me to this suburb, which she has had issues with since the day we arrived. But in those days we thought we'd have children, and she could see the plus side of living in a walking community where even the local grocery store was only a mile away. It was later, after it became clear that no children were forthcoming, that she grew testy about our location and pressed me to move. By the time we had exhausted all options, including years of fertility treatments, we had been in our house for fifteen years and I was very comfortable. Every time she complained I reminded her how much we were saving on the commute and how pleasant it was to walk down to the lake in the warmer months. By the time Creighton came into the picture, I was only two years from retirement and I was begging her to hold out a little longer. My primary concern was the real-estate market, which had tanked. Our house was worth half what we'd paid for it fifteen years before.

The next day after school, Tina Stewart came up to me with a petition. "This is the greatest challenge of our times," she said in a voice that could have been a computer simulation. She was wearing a tight blue sweater and a skirt so short I wondered whether it was part of her cheerleading outfit.

"Excuse me?" I said.

"Did you know that the governor wants us to join the Schools of Choice initiative?" She leaned over my desk.

"I did not." I sat back in my chair to create more space between us.

"If we're not filled to capacity, he wants us to open our doors to students from," she cupped her hands around her mouth and whispered, "*neighboring districts.*"

"Interesting," I said.

"Well, even if it weren't *dangerous*, we're entitled to local control. We give our own money to these schools to supplement the state-allocated funding. It's not fair to us to have other people freeloading."

"Hmm," I said. "I'm going to give that some thought and get back to you."

"I have to turn this in soon," she said, straightening up and receding from the desktop. "So please get back to me fast."

The next week in class, we moved on to a chapter on the welfare system, a comparison between the United States and the United Kingdom.

I lectured for the first half of the class, and then as soon as I was through, Creighton raised his hand. I looked around the room for an alternative but, as usual, no one else had anything to offer.

"Rich people are rich because they've done something to earn it," he said. "And poor people have become too dependent on the system. The reason they never get anywhere is they keep working the system. They refuse to man up and get a job or an education."

"I'm not sure it's that simple," I said.

Katie Reed, an accomplished clarinetist and chess player, raised her hand. "Lots of people try to earn money, but it's like if one thing goes wrong, they're in trouble. Like if they're working at McDonald's or something and they break their leg, then they are out of work and the bills pile up and they can never get out from under them."

"There's more to it than that," Creighton said. He sat ramrod straight in his chair. When other people spoke, he didn't turn around to face them. He remained face forward staring at me throughout every discussion. I found it a little disconcerting.

Sonya raised her hand. "I don't know what his problem is," she said, jabbing her pointer finger in Creighton's direction. "But what Katie said is true. My cousin Rita, she had a job at the mall and then the store closed, and she had no way to pay the rent, and she had to go look for a new job and pay for daycare, and she got in something deep and now she ain't never gonna be able to pay off everything."

"That is not the problem," Creighton said to me. "The problem is the big-screen TV and the leather sectional her cousin bought on credit." He laughed.

"She did not!" Sonya shouted, rising up out of her chair.

"OK. OK," I said, waving at Sonya to sit back down. The football players straightened up in their seats and the girls in the third row, the ones who twirled their hair and surreptitiously checked their smartphones during class, looked up, engaging with the discussion for the first time. When I looked at Tina Stewart she rolled her eyes.

"Creighton, I would like to have a word with you after class," I said.

Sonya sat back down.

Though I had more to say about the welfare dilemma, I didn't think it wise to pursue that subject, so I asked the class to turn to the section on macro- versus microeconomics.

It has not been easy living in the suburbs without participating in any of the requisite parental activities like Little League and waffle-cone Wednesday. Long ago, Monica and I got into the habit of taking leisurely evening walks to ameliorate the loneliness that descended during the hours of four to seven, when we might have been checking homework or sitting down for a family dinner.

That night I brought up Creighton again.

"He probably feels like a fish out of water," Monica said.

We were walking past a soccer match and had stopped to watch. The children were small and seemed to have no idea what they were supposed to do. A red-faced coach kept shouting for them to "move, move!"

"That's no excuse," I said. "Some of the kids might have similar political leanings, but they would never be so strident. If a white kid said all of the stuff he's saying in class, he'd be kicked out of school."

"And yet they say it among themselves, don't they?" Monica said, rolling her eyes.

She was right—that kind of talk did happen, and I admitted it. "But not often," I added.

"You and I can agree to disagree," Monica said. "I warned you from day one that living in a place like this would warp you. I should have made you leave, retirement package or no retirement package."

As if Monica wasn't alienated enough, we ran into Tina Stewart's mother, Missy, at a booster-club fundraiser that weekend. Missy had been a classmate of mine at Fox Grove back in the eighties, and if anything, she was even meaner and more self-righteous than she'd been back then. There had even been a rumor that she'd had a hand in getting a good friend of mine, Gary Smith, expelled for selling drugs. Gary was a scholarship student. He wanted to be a rocket scientist and he was smart enough to do it. He was so distraught at losing his scholarship he jumped into the Detroit River. Luckily someone pulled him out. I do think Missy had something to do with Gary's expulsion and for that reason I steer clear of her. However, I know better than to display any antagonism. She is the type of person who would have made me pay for that.

Missy saw us the minute we walked in the door and ran toward us in a too-tight pink suit and matching shoes, her blond hair fanning out around the back of her neck like a bushy tail. She barely paused to say hello before demanding to know why I hadn't signed the petition about Schools of Choice.

"I'm not sure how I feel about it," I said.

"Do you know that we are one of only fifteen percent of school districts in the state that haven't agreed to Schools of Choice? The governor is going to try to force our hand if we don't band together. They have no idea what we're up against down here in this part of the state."

"What are we up against?" Monica said.

I knew from Monica's tone that she was already fuming, and I ran through a list of possible escape plans in my head.

"Oh, you know, Monica—crime, drugs, poor grades, kids without families. Trouble, in short." Missy looked down at

Monica from her great height—the woman must have been six foot one to Monica's five foot two.

"That's not true of all the students," Monica said.

"You don't know, honey. I used to work as a social worker down there. I used to test them." Missy shook her head as if greatly dismayed by the memory.

"And?" Monica said.

"And, well, it was very sad."

"What was sad?" Monica's nose had gone red at the tip like a teapot ready to blow.

"Well, the test scores were pathetic. Really." Missy tilted her head and gave us a look that must have meant something, but I couldn't figure out what. Later, Monica said she'd had a Botox injection, which made it impossible for her to move her face.

"All of the test scores? All of them? Are you trying to tell me that an entire group of people tested poorly?" Monica said.

"Pretty much."

"Oh, give me a break!" Monica said.

"I was there. I know what they do! They wouldn't even give their own children pencils! We had to sneak them pencils out of the supply closet. Why, one kid even tried to assault me. Another boy had to hold him back."

"So what about the boy who tried to stop him? Doesn't he deserve to go to a good school? Does he deserve to be lumped in with everyone else?" Monica's voice had risen and I took her arm and pressed on it to remind her where we were.

"You don't know," Missy said. "You sit on your wicker settee and you have no idea what goes on down there."

"My wicker settee? What are you talking about? I work at the food bank! You are unbelievable! You know what? I'm not going to listen to this anymore." She leaned forward and got as close to Missy's face as she could without resorting to tiptoes. "I don't think you have any idea what a—what an—*asshole* you are."

After she'd said it, she turned and hurried off down the hall. Later, I found her in the guest bathroom shaking. Missy had stormed out of the room after her. She must have left the party immediately as I didn't see her again that night, thank God, and we left ourselves as quickly as we could.

I was worried about my job after that incident. As PTO president, Missy wielded a big stick. On Sunday, I begged Monica to write an apology and she did it for me, but she wasn't happy.

"Can't I just say, 'I'm sorry—what I meant to say was you are a racist?'"

I told her no. I reminded her that after retirement we could move wherever she wanted.

"I can't wait to get out of here," she said, and handed me the sealed envelope. "I hate it! I hate it! I hate it! Two years seems like an eternity."

That Monday, I had to pull Creighton aside again after he riled some kids in the hallway by saying something monstrous.

"Creighton," I said. "Not everyone here is a racist."

"Well, I can't blame them if they are."

"How can you say that?"

"My feeling is that everyone is angry and afraid. And if they say they aren't, they're lying."

"I'm not," I said.

"Sure you are," he said. "You lock your car when you go downtown."

"Well, that's because it's a high-crime area."

"Yeah, and what color are the criminals?" he said.

"Not all of them."

"Most."

"I don't even know if that's statistically accurate." I pulled a Kleenex out of the box on my desk and began to shred it.

"Don't feel bad about it, Mr. Clarke. There are lots of crazy things going on in the world. Like the Jews, for instance. I'm not sure what the Jews are up to. It's like they've gone Rambo over there in Israel. And the Muslims—when I see one of those camel jockeys coming my way, I just cross the street. Those guys are nuts!"

He had made it to the threshold of the doorway before I was able to speak.

"Creighton!" My hands were balled into fists. I felt blood rushing to my face.

He turned around.

"If I ever hear *anything* like that coming out of your mouth again, I will tell the principal and have your parents called in too. For your information, my wife is Jewish."

"OK," he said, but he said it like someone says OK if you tell them you borrowed a sheet of their loose-leaf paper. He couldn't, in short, have cared less.

That night, Monica asked about Creighton. I didn't want to wound her by telling her that on top of everything else he was an anti-Semite. Instead, I shook my head and said, "I think the boy is very confused."

"We have no idea," she said. "Just remember that. We're white. We can't even remember what it was like to be oppressed. We don't have any idea what it would be like to be black and go to school in this town."

I decided to ask a student named Jack Smith what the general consensus was about Creighton. He was popular, had grown up in the area, and seemed to know everyone. I resolved to do it covertly while he was asking me for help after school the following afternoon. It proved easier than I expected.

Jack was writing a paper on cost-benefit analysis, a basic concept that, for some reason, he was having trouble comprehending.

"Jack," I said. "This is similar to something Creighton said the other day . . ."

"Sheesh, Mr. Clarke," Jack said. "I don't know what's wrong with him."

"What do you mean?"

Jack shook his head. "I feel bad for him, I really do, it can't be easy . . . but I mean, he is one crazy—" He stopped just in time. "Sorry, I mean . . ."

"Why do you say that?"

"You ought to hear him on Facebook. He says things . . . Honestly, no one can stand him." He flipped his head and swiped at his bangs so he could see me.

"What did he say?"

Jack shook his head and his bangs went right back over his eyes. "If I told you, you would die. I'm telling you, he'd be expelled. Let's just say that if that guy wasn't black, I would swear he was a white supremacist."

"Where do you think he's getting these ideas?" I said.

"Well, I heard his dad is like head of some real conservative church. Some wackadoodle group. Creighton sits with these kids at lunch ... we call them the Nazis."

"Come on! The Nazis? Isn't that a little extreme?"

"That's what we call them. They're just ... I mean, they might as well have swastikas and shit—and stuff. He sits with them. The black kids stare him down at lunch. They can't believe he's associating with those guys and the white kids stare him down too because they're thinking, what? Are you crazy? It's like eating lunch with the Ku Klux Klan."

"Very strange," I said. "And they let him sit at the table? I mean, if they hate everyone?"

"But that's the thing, Mr. Clarke. Creighton is like way meaner than those guys. He calls them crackers, rednecks, trailer-park trash, gutter bunnies, all sorts of stuff, and they just laugh. They must get off on it. That kid is never going to get into college. If any college saw what he was saying on Facebook, they would be like, um, no thank you."

The next day I was creating a circular flowchart when Tina Stewart knocked on my door.

"My mom said you might sign the petition now," she said. This time she was wearing a low-cut purple minidress with three-inch heels. If I had a daughter, I would not let her out of the house in a getup like that.

"She did?"

"She said you might have had a change of heart after what happened," Tina said.

"Why would she think that?"

"I don't know, Mr. Clarke." Tina shrugged and opened her eyes wide. "She thought you might not want word getting out about certain people who were very impolite."

I sat back in my chair. I've been teaching for a long time, but I'd never been threatened before.

"Well, this is something," I said. "Tell me, Tina, why do you feel so strongly about this issue?"

"I know it may not seem very Christian, Mr. Clarke, but we are just trying to protect our community. I want to raise my kids here. I want to raise my kids with other nice, wholesome people. I don't want the neighborhood going to rot and when I think about what they're trying to force us into, well, I get very, very angry about it."

There is nothing a teacher enjoys more than a well-behaved, enthusiastic pupil. In this suburb, whatever its flaws, the children are generally tractable. I am ashamed, but I must admit I shared some of Tina's fears, however base I believed her to be.

"I'll think about it," I said. "And get back to you tomorrow or the next day."

When I handed back the petition, her fake smile hit me like a dart.

I started feeling apprehensive whenever Creighton raised his hand. What would come out of his mouth next? On channel one every morning students on the journalism track broadcast on closed-circuit TV. We were subjected to editorials on everything from ranting monologues about unrest in the Middle East to the state of the lavatories and the lack of chocolate pudding at lunch.

One morning, Creighton and his classmates filed in just as the perky, pigtailed host was bantering away about Schools of

Choice. She introduced two students—Tina Stewart, in another audacious costume, and Max Kanin—who were sitting in armchairs opposite each other. I couldn't bear it. I turned off the television and opened my book. Creighton raised his hand.

"I would like to hear that discussion about Schools of Choice," he said.

"Not today," I said. I tried to say it with a stern tone, and I gave him quite a look as well, but he didn't notice.

"I just have to say that I am very worried about it. I don't know about my classmates, but I really feel that if we let them in, they'll bring the entire district down."

"I'm not sure that will be the case," I said.

"Sure it will," he said. "Have you ever been to one of their schools?"

"No," I said.

"Do you know what they do there?"

Sonya raised her hand. "Who is they?" she said.

"Those kids in the city," Creighton said.

"You mean those black kids?" she said.

"Those kids who are economically disadvantaged, those kids whose parents are riding the system, those kids who don't know their thumb from their—"

"You are such an asshole!" Sonya screamed, slamming her fist down on her desk.

"Hey, hey," I said.

"I don't know why you're mad at me," Creighton said. "I'm just telling the truth. They really are animals."

A small collective gasp sounded out around the room. Sonya stood up, gathered her books, and marched out of the room. The other students stared at her with mouths open and eyes wide; several in the back started giggling nervously.

"That is absolutely inappropriate, Creighton. Just because people are impoverished doesn't mean they are animals, and I think we've learned on more than one occasion during our studies of economics here in this classroom that it is not very easy to pull yourself up out of poverty. I think you need to go to the office right this minute."

"With hard work," Creighton said, getting up and putting his clipboard in his briefcase, "it can be done. And if it can be done, there is no excuse for not doing it."

Tom Ryan, the principal, gave Creighton a warning. The next time, he said, he would have no choice but to suspend him.

I decided to ask some of the other faculty members about Creighton.

"I had him for math," Mary Blanchett said. "Very well behaved. Very bright."

"Did he ever say anything controversial?" I said.

"Not a thing!" she said. "Why are you asking?"

"Well, economics is a different kind of class. We talk about society and what's going on around us, and Creighton is very outspoken."

"Well, I don't blame him at all," Mary said. "His people have had a hard time of it, haven't they? I mean, they've been oppressed. I don't wonder he has a lot to say."

The next day, I was sitting at my desk during first lunch when my pencil cup started to rattle. A pounding sound was coming through the floor. I got up and walked to my door, opened it, and looked up and down the hall. No one was in the hallway, but people were yelling in the lunchroom three doors down and I could hear utensils banging against trays and the stomping of feet. Dana Rowen, the physics teacher, peeked out of her room across the hall. "What's going on?" she said.

"It's coming from the lunchroom," I said.

In the lunchroom, students were standing on their seats. Several were actually up on the tables, stomping their feet and booing.

Behind us several other teachers came through the door and we stood in a cluster trying to figure out what was going on. Tom Ryan appeared and pushed his way through the crowd. The other teachers, myself included, followed him into the center of the room. He took out a whistle and blew it several times. It was so shrill it silenced the crowd instantaneously. Everyone reflexively put their hands up over their ears. Where had he purchased such an ear-shattering whistle? Maybe it was something that principals kept on hand for emergencies.

In the center of the room stood Max Kanin and Creighton LaMott, in what appeared to be a face-off. Max's shirt was askew, hanging off of one shoulder, and the left side of his face was red as if he'd been struck. Creighton was holding his stomach.

"What is going on here?" Tom said.

Max pointed a finger at Creighton. "He is a terrible person. He is a terrible, terrible person!"

All around the room, the other children started to clap and stomp their feet—everyone hooting and booing and pointing their fingers at Creighton. It was frightening.

"What happened?" Tom said.

"I said something last night on Facebook about being completely broke, and he wrote back, 'You are such a Jew.'"

Tom looked over at Creighton, who gave his customary shrug. "At least I didn't offer to round up the cattle cars."

There was a split second when no one moved. I had time to look around the room at all of the horrified faces and see that even Tina Stewart's bright-red mouth was agape.

"You are out of here, Creighton!" Tom shouted, pointing toward the door. "Out! Out! Out! Out of my school!"

At that news, there was a general whoop of joy. Kids from one end of the room to the other started high-fiving.

Tom blew the whistle again.

"That is enough!" he yelled.

He motioned vigorously to Creighton and they headed toward the door.

"Serves you right, you racist pig!" someone screamed.

I looked through the crowd and saw that it was Sonya who had shouted. An enormous boy with a buzz cut gave her a high five.

Just before Creighton reached the door, he stopped and turned around. Tom took hold of his arm and turned him back toward the exit, but Creighton shook him off. Then he put his palms together and bowed to us, holding the pose for what seemed like a long time. Finally, he straightened back up.

"If you look the right way, you can see," he said.

It has taken me a long time to get over it. More than a year has passed since Creighton was expelled. Rumors fly about what happened to him, but the truth is, no one knows. Soon afterward his family sold the house, and within a couple of months they were gone. Some people said California, others said Indiana, where he had family. Every now and then I Google him, but nothing has come up so far. His Facebook page remains inactive.

Monica and I have had a rough time of it. She found out what happened to Creighton and right after that she saw my name on the petition about Schools of Choice reprinted in the local paper. I had rationalized the act by telling myself that while signing the petition wouldn't swing the vote, not signing it might cost me my job.

"You sold your soul," Monica said when she saw it.

For several weeks after that she was morose and withdrawn. She watched a lot of television. When I tried to talk to her, she either didn't respond or nodded perfunctorily even though I knew she wasn't listening to a word I said. I knew I had asked her to put up with a lot, including living in a place she disliked, but I told myself I wouldn't have done it if the job market had been better, if I wasn't so close to the finish line, if I could have thought of a way around it.

One day about three weeks after, I couldn't take it anymore, and I sat down next to her while she was reading on the couch. When she ignored me, I took her hand gently in mine. I could tell she wanted to withdraw it. I asked her if she was ever going to forgive me.

"I wish it was that easy," she said, without looking up from her book.

"What do you mean?"

"I forgive you," she said. "I just don't like you anymore."

the

vagaries

of love

❧

2007

The first night of the Caribbean cruise, Missy and Alice are in their respective beds at two in the morning, listening to Stephanie hurl in the bathroom, when Missy announces that she has set her alarm for 7:00 a.m. in order to go to chapel before their first excursion.

"You've got to be kidding," Alice says. She has not had a cigarette in years, and her mouth, after a long night in the ship's casino, feels like it contains something a plumber might extract from a clogged drain.

"I've changed," Missy says, shoving her suitcase under the adjacent twin bed. "I'm getting old and I need the Lord."

The cabin is tiny, and they've had to cram everything under the beds just to be able to stand. Now that housekeeping has pulled out

Alice's sofa bed, they'll have to climb over it to get to the balcony. But at least they've sprung for a balcony. Without it, Alice would feel totally hemmed in. The gentle motion of the boat and the thrumming makes her heart rev. But, then again, what doesn't these days?

"When did you become religious?" Alice says. "I don't remember you ever going to church."

"I've found this great community church," Missy says. "They serve lattes and you can wear anything you want. It really helped me get through that time after Jim's affair. I pray all the time now."

Alice fights the urge to say something snide. She's changed too and she hopes for the better. It has been two months since she switched to the new medication, and, prior to this trip, she actually felt it had been working. But seeing Missy might knock her down a rung or two. The cruise was Stephanie's idea, and Alice reminds herself that they are doing it for her. She's just lost her husband—a heart attack at forty-two—out of the blue. She begged them to go on the cruise with her. How great to get the old college roommates back together, she'd said. And no one had argued.

Stephanie emerges from the bathroom with a towel wrapped around her midriff and another wound turban-style on her head.

"I feel like shit," Stephanie says, squeezing past their beds and flopping down on the sofa bed. "I'm glad I don't run into you two more often. If I did, I'd probably be dead by now."

"Missy set her alarm for seven," Alice says, looking over at Missy, her disapproval barely masked.

"I'll try to be quiet. I won't wake you up." Missy has shut her eyes.

"No, wake me up," Stephanie says. "I need to work out, or maybe I should pray too . . ."

Alice thinks of the line from the Bible, "Whither thou goest I will follow." Everyone in high school looked up to Missy; now Missy has all of the things the other girls aspired to: a rich investment banker for a husband, three beautiful kids, a large house, membership at the country club.

Stephanie's life has been harder. First, she was married first to Arnie, a pilot, who bragged that flight school was all about "getting laid." Then to a country-music singer named Snell Hawkins who was well known in Montgomery, Alabama, but nowhere else. Before he died, he could muster up enough enthusiasm to run through his repertoire but had taken to sleeping all day. He'd passed in his sleep, and Stephanie didn't ask for an autopsy. She didn't want to know if other "substances" were involved. "If I had kids," she said. "I would have had to have an autopsy, but luckily I don't." This was the first and only time she'd described it as "lucky." Not having kids had always been a big bone of contention between Snell and Stephanie. Snell's mother was bipolar and he'd never wanted to pass on that gene.

Alice has just started thinking about what to do after the kids go to college, but she hasn't decided on anything. Things seem to be looking up in Detroit. Or, at least, that's the way Ed sees it. For the last ten years he's been running her father's tool-and-die company, and the whole time, despite evidence to the contrary, he's been telling her that things are looking up. Sometimes when they're joking around, she calls him "the mayor," because when it comes to Detroit, it would be an understatement to say he's wearing rose-colored glasses. This, she believes, is the main reason she married him, because he is three-fourths full most of the time. They have two kids and live in a much more liberal suburb than the stodgy one on the east side where she grew up. The four-bed-room home is not nearly as ostentatious as the estate she grew up on, but then, not as unhappy either. Their life is quiet, which is good because Alice still has what she likes to refer to as "epi-sodes." Her therapist, Dr. Evalyn Wu, believes that Alice is suffer-ing from post-traumatic stress disorder, and that for many years when the kids were younger she'd buried these bad experiences so that she wouldn't come unhinged. Now that she has more time on her hands, all of the things she never coped with are coming back to haunt her. Her sister's death, her mother's defection (with the tennis pro), her senior year of college. Her sister's death is what Dr. Wu deems "the inciting incident." She says it makes sense that after mother left, Alice gave up on a master's degree, started read-ing poetry, taking long hikes, progressing from pot to coke and beyond. She believes Alice uses her inherited wealth as a means to seal herself off from life, and although this feels true, Alice is amazed at how easily Dr. Wu labels her behavior, as if putting it in the proper box means that eventually she'll be able (or want to) snap the lid on her past for good.

"I was just thinking about Mike Gallagher," Missy says. "I wonder what happened to him?"

"He became a park ranger," Alice says.

Missy laughs. "You've got to be kidding!" she says. "Do you keep in touch with him?"

Alice shakes her head. She hasn't talked to Mike since col-lege. A Facebook friend told her he was working as a park ranger somewhere out west, maybe even Alaska. It's surprising mostly because it's exactly what he once told her he wanted to do. How many people can say that?

"What about the Fish Bowl," Missy says, her eyes still closed. "Remember that dump?" The Fish Bowl was the name of the living room in the Delt House where they held all of their parties. The room had been christened in honor of the 200-gallon fish tank where the Delts kept the goldfish that were swallowed whole during pledge week and sometimes at parties.

"What about it?" Stephanie says, having assumed the exact same position as Missy, eyes closed, covers pulled up to her neck.

"All the great parties we had there," Missy says. "Remember, Alice?"

"Not really," Alice lies. She waits a beat, but there's no response from Missy. "What made you think of the Fish Bowl?"

In answer, there's a small snore from Missy and Stephanie giggles. "See you tomorrow," she says.

※

Senior year, the week before graduation, Alice was in the midst of yet another breakup with Mike. The summer before senior year, she'd almost broken up with him, but then her mother ran off with the tennis pro, and Alice got drunk one night in October and after much cajoling, ended up in Mike's bed again, where he listened to her lamenting the loss of her family until dawn. It wasn't clear to her later whether he was listening or he was just happy to look like he was listening because he had lured her to his room and the longer he listened, the more lines he was able to coax out of her.

Ever since they had gotten back together in the fall, she'd been arriving at parties only to be confronted by one or another of Mike's solemn-looking fraternity brothers: "Alice, would you mind taking him home? He got hold of a bat and we had to wrestle it away from him." It wasn't that Mike was likely to beat anyone up; he was too good-natured for that. But if he swung it drunkenly, he might bop a passerby on the head.

The walk home sometimes took hours, Alice navigating Mike down the narrow streets with frequent stops to pee or lie down on the ground. When she finally steered him back to his dorm and into bed, she sometimes sat at his desk smoking and watching him, his half-open eyes fascinating to her. She did not know, until a nurse told her years later, that alcohol poisoning can cause the oculomotor system to shut down.

During Senior Week, this same rescue scenario had played out yet again and Alice had walked back to the party after depositing Mike in bed, determined to end it, make a clean break, get on with her summer internship at WABC television in Manhattan and journalism school at Columbia in the fall. It was a balmy night. As Alice approached the Fish Bowl, she could hear the music pulsing and the feet pounding on the sagging wooden floor. The Episcopal Church's spires were illuminated in the moonlight, the whole campus appearing gothic and surreal, like the set of a film noir.

Just as she was about to cross the street, a figure waved to her from underneath the ancient oak tree on the church lawn. She walked toward the person, who turned out to be Ziggy Monroe, a fraternity brother of Mike's. He was sitting with his back against the tree, smoking a joint. Across the street, the noise from the Fish Bowl amplified every time a reveler spilled out into the night.

"What are you doing here?" Alice said, walking up to him. "You're being pretty obvious with that," she added, pointing to the joint.

"What are they going to do about it now?" Ziggy said. "We're graduating in two days."

Alice could think of a few things, but said nothing. Ziggy had always been an outlier in Mike's fraternity. She'd never really gotten a sense of him. Though he was good-looking, tall and dark-haired with broad shoulders—some girls thought he looked like Keanu Reeves—he hardly ever dated, and when he did, it was always someone from his hometown who no one knew. Ziggy was a poet, another reason Alice had never spoken to him. She was a journalism major, a world apart from the creative writing department where students made up stories and poems, all figments of their imaginations, with no basis in truth.

"Have a seat," Ziggy said, patting the ground next to him.

Alice didn't want to be rude, though she desperately wanted to return to the party and have fun for once.

"I've been wanting to ask you this for years," he said, glancing at her out of the corner of his eye, as if reluctant.

"What?"

"Why do you date that guy?"

"You mean Mike, your fraternity brother?" Alice said.

"I guess you could call him that," he said, toking his joint. "He's a good guy, don't get me wrong, it's just I don't see what you get out of it. Every night you drag him home like a sack of potatoes."

Alice was glad he couldn't see her blushing. She looked across the street at the party. "Who can explain the vagaries of love?" she said.

Ziggy laughed. "The vagaries of love?"

Alice smiled. "I was trying to sound poetic."

For the next half hour they sat and talked about school and what life would be like after it. Alice was ready to leave; Ziggy was not. He did not seem to have a plan. He said his parents were fine with that. Alice said her father would kill her if she didn't know what she was doing by now.

"He sent me to college," she said. "I'm sure he expects me to get something out of it." It was not true at all, and right after she said it she wondered why she had and where the whole notion had come from. Her father couldn't care less about the tuition bills or whether she ever got a job. His wife was living in Paris with another man and he was suffering from heart problems brought on by her departure. He had not been a great parent, but he was far from a tyrant. One time earlier on in college, he'd tried to convince her to become a banker, but after that failed he'd never voiced any expectations of Alice at all.

Ziggy said his parents were "flexible," that they'd been hippies and that they still lived off the grid in upstate New York. They wanted him to find himself. His plan was to drive across country after graduation, staying with friends along the way.

Alice rolled her eyes. "Let me ask you a question," she said.

"Shoot."

"What are you going to do with an English degree? Are you really going to be a poet?"

"Probably not. But I have emerged from this institution with some pretty great pickup lines."

"Let me hear one," Alice said. She breathed out the smoke and felt for a second as if she was levitating. She pressed her hands into the earth and then lay back, looking up at the sky.

Ziggy held his hand out to her. "OK, here goes. This is kind of cheesy, but for you to get the full effect, you have to sit back up."

"OK," Alice said. Sitting up proved harder than she thought it would be.

"Now face me," Ziggy said. "Pretend we're sitting at The Rambler, OK?"

"Never been there," Alice said. "Is that in town?"

Ziggy nodded. "OK, well then, pretend you're sitting at some other bar and I come up and sit next to you and we talk for a while and then, when the moment is right, I take your hands and I look into your eyes." For effect he leaned in and looked into Alice's eyes. She laughed.

"Then I say:

How many loved your moments of glad grace,
And loved your beauty with love false or true;
But one man loved the pilgrim soul in you,
And loved the sorrows of your changing face."

Alice wanted to laugh, but he kept looking at her and she felt something else she couldn't identify. The poem or verse or whatever it was, was beautiful. She wished that instead of some random guy spouting a pickup line, someone would say it to her in earnest. Mike, in his current state, would never say it. She had wasted years on him, and would never get them back. Why had she done it? She could not imagine a scenario where anyone on the planet would ever recite poetry to her. She could not imagine a scenario where she would believe the person even if they did. Something, she suddenly realized, was terribly wrong with the way she was living her life. She let go of Ziggy's hands and stood up. At the same time, she heard someone shout. It was Missy; she'd just come out of the party with Stephanie.

"Great job," she said to Ziggy. "You've really got that down. No girl will be able to resist."

When she reached her friends, Missy took her arm. "What were you talking to Ziggy about?" she said.

"Nothing," Alice said. "He's kind of a tool." She was high, having trouble catching her breath. She knew she was imagining it, but it always happened when she smoked pot. One night a few months before, she'd frozen in front the television for hours; breathing felt like trying to suck air in through a straw. At the clinic the next day, the doctor said that her lungs were fine, but she was suffering from paranoia. Later, when it started happening all the time, they called it a panic disorder.

As they walked, Stephanie babbled on about the night and the dancing and the two couples she'd seen hooking up outside the bathroom and one guy who was throwing up in the bushes, into which his baseball cap had fallen.

"When he was done, he just picked it up, dumped out the puke, and put it back on his head," she said, opening her mouth to simulate gagging.

"That is sick," Missy said.

When they reached the apartment, Missy turned to Alice. "You know I have to tell you something," she said. "Did you know Ziggy and I hook up sometimes?"

"Really?" Alice said. Missy hooked up with a lot of people, but she had no idea Ziggy was one of them.

"I didn't think you were his type," Stephanie said.

"Nice," Missy said.

"I meant you're not from his hometown," Stephanie said, horrified at having offended her.

"I know what you meant," Missy sighed. "It's no big deal. It's just a sometimes thing."

"Oh," Alice said.

"I just haven't said anything because . . . well, it hasn't been . . . I'm not sure what to make of it," Missy said with a shrug.

Stephanie lit a cigarette and leaned against the railing, wobbling slightly. Alice fumbled with the key, but got it into the lock.

"Watch it, Steph," Missy said as Steph stumbled into the house in front of them. "The thing is," she continued, putting a hand on Alice's arm to stop her, "I wouldn't like it if you got together with him. I just wanted you to know that in case you were considering it."

"Well, I'm not," Alice said.

"Good," Missy said.

❧

The ladies in Missy's tennis league have all told her that in The Sunset Bar on Maho Beach is the place to see and be seen. The next morning, right before the boat docks, Missy goes to church and Stephanie shames Alice into an hour on the elliptical machine. In the cafeteria line, they all fill their plates with fruit. Later, they catch a taxi to the beach. The countryside is rocky and deserted and much less scenic than Alice expected. It is the beginning of January and though Alice had assumed it would be sunny, it turns out not to be true. It is sprinkling and too early in the morning for sunbathers. Stephanie shows Missy and Alice a YouTube video of the beach and impossibly beautiful people dancing and laughing and squirting each other with Champagne.

"We'll fit right in," Alice says, receiving a sharp look from Missy, who seems to bite her tongue to keep from saying, "Some of us can still fit in."

The beach is deserted. At the bar a lone bartender, a young man with dark, curly hair and a black T-shirt that reads "TAKE IT OFF," sits on a stool cleaning a glass and staring with glassy, unfocused eyes at the sea. All of the chairs are lined up under a round white tent. White sofas are clumped together in haphazard arrangements. An older couple lounges on one, sipping coffee. They wear matching White Sox hats and bright-blue Bermuda shorts, obviously Americans. The sky is gunmetal gray.

"St. Martin enjoys three-hundred-plus days of sunshine per year, according to the guidebook," Stephanie says, flipping through it.

"What are we going to do here all day?" Missy says, clutching her Prada bag and looking around.

"We're going to get drunk," Stephanie says, setting the book and her backpack on the ground next to the couch. She walks over to the baby-faced bartender.

"This isn't what I expected," Missy says, lowering herself down onto one of the white couches. It's a delicate procedure because her heels are so high. "I thought we were going to get some sun."

"I never go out in the sun," Alice says. "For some reason I can't take it anymore."

"I can't live without it," Missy says.

Stephanie returns with three mimosas and passes Alice the cigarettes.

"I can't believe we're smoking," Alice says, shaking her head.

The bartender is talking with a small man in loose-fitting jeans and a striped poncho who keeps looking over at them. His movements are wiry and languid. A really bad cliché of an aging playboy.

"Oh, God, please don't come over here," Alice says.

"Why not?" Missy says, waving. "It will be more exciting than sitting here by ourselves all day."

The man waves back and ambles toward them as slowly and deliberately as a panther.

"What are you beautiful ladies up to on this beautiful day?" he says.

Alice almost laughs. Stephanie looks at Missy and giggles. Missy says, "Everyone told us to come to this beach, but I have to say this is a little disappointing."

"My name is Oscar," he says. "You are disappointed because it is too early in the day. Everyone is asleep and won't be recovered until much later this afternoon."

"And what do you do, Oscar?" Stephanie says, flipping her hair and inhaling deeply.

Alice is glad that she has sunglasses on and no one can see her rolling her eyes. She wanted to take the daytrip to Saba—the "unspoiled queen" of the Caribbean where she could scuba dive. But Stephanie and Missy thought the ferry ride was too long and besides, Stephanie, the claustrophobic one, freaked out last time she tried to put on the diving helmet. Now there is nothing to do but sit back and watch her middle-aged friends flirt shamelessly with Oscar, who eggs them on.

"How old would you say we are?" Missy says.

"Missy!" Alice says.

"What?" she says. "I'm just curious."

"I don't see your age," Oscar says. "I see your soul. I see it in your eyes."

"Ahh," Stephanie says. "Isn't that nice?"

"All except for her," he says, pointing at Alice. "She wears those dark glasses and I can't see her soul."

"She doesn't have one," Missy says, standing up. Then, perhaps because she sounds angrier than she meant to, she adds, "I have to go to the bathroom."

Alice follows her. The bathroom is painted a bright Caribbean blue. On the walls are pictures of women dancing. They all appear to be having the time of their lives.

Missy goes into a stall and slams the door, which confirms Alice's suspicion. "What did you mean by that?" she says.

"I just meant that back then it didn't seem like you had one," Missy says, her voice muffled. "You didn't give a shit about anyone but yourself."

Alice looks into the mirror. Her eyes are like cartoon eyes, enormous and shot through with red streaks. She turns around to glare at Missy's stall.

"I'm taking this cruise for Stephanie, but make no mistake," Missy continues. "I never got over what you did. Did you ever even feel bad about it? And what about Mike? Did you even think about how he'd . . ." She doesn't finish, or she finishes but the toilet flushes. Either way, Alice misses it.

❦

That night after the talk with Ziggy, Alice went straight to bed. If she brushed her teeth, she had no memory of doing it. She never heard the small window in her dorm room sliding open or Ziggy crawling through it. She didn't hear anything at all. But the next morning when she opened her eyes, there he was beside her. At the sight of him, she shot out of bed as if he were a venomous snake and stood by the door with her hand over her mouth. She looked down to make sure she was still dressed. She leaned over and looked in the mirror. Her face wasn't chafed, her lips didn't look bruised or swollen. She felt between her legs. She wasn't sore. She saw that he was also fully dressed and that he was lying on top of her covers, not under them.

She was just trying to figure out how to wake him up and sneak him out when a loud pounding started up outside her room. She opened her door a smidge. Across the hall Stephanie opened hers as well.

"Who could that be?" Stephanie said. The pounding was coming from the front door.

Missy came out into the hall in her glasses, wearing gray sweat shorts and a matching gray T-shirt. Alice quickly closed her door. Then she pressed her ear to it.

"Is Alice here?" a voice said.

Shit, Alice thought. She hadn't even done anything.

On the bed, Ziggy rolled over toward the wall and put the pillow over his head.

Alice opened the door and slid through it, shutting it tightly behind her. It was Mark Angler, one of Mike's fraternity brothers. She would just have to tell the truth. She'd gone to sleep and Ziggy, the weirdo, had crawled through her window. But Mark looked terrible. His eyes were red, and his brown hair, normally matted, was standing up in tufts all over his head. He was wearing a white undershirt and boxer shorts. He must have crossed campus in his underwear. Missy and Alice stared at his underwear.

"What the hell are you doing?" Missy said.

Mark ignored her. He turned to Alice and took her hands. "It's Mike," he said. "Jimmy went in to get something. From Mike's desk, I guess, and he found him. He OD'd. They think they have him stabilized." He took in a breath. "I ran over here so you wouldn't just hear about it from anyone else."

Later, Alice did not remember anything that happened at the hospital. She didn't remember Mike finally coming to or watching his parents arrive and arrange for transport to the rehab facility. She didn't remember taking the sedatives Missy handed her or anything else that transpired the rest of the day before her father arrived and drove her back to Michigan. Later everything remained a blur except for the walk to the car that morning. It felt like the Bataan Death March, which she had just finished studying in her World War II class. Missy had enlisted Mark to help. Together, they'd dragged Alice, Stephanie on one side, Mark on the other, to the parking lot, a quarter of a mile away down a wooded path. Missy had led the way. The whole time, Alice kept her eyes fixed on Missy's enormous key chain. She was holding it in her right hand and whipping it rhythmically against her bare leg. When they finally reached the car, Ziggy, who must have followed them, tried to slide in beside Alice, but Missy held her hand up like a stop sign and said, in a voice shot through with venom, "I think we'll take it from here, Ziggy."

Back at home, Alice lay in the living room on the bright-pink silk couch (her mother's last purchase before she'd deserted), numb for days on end. She flicked through television shows but could not follow anything. She rolled over and stared at the spines of the coffee-table books, the same ones that had been there since she was a child—*Classics of the Silent Film Era* and *Masterpieces of The Metropolitan Museum of Art*. Her father sat across from her in his easy chair, reading Louis L'Amour novels, his slippered feet on the ottoman. Miss Powers was the only one member of the old household cleaning staff who still worked for her father since his tool-and-die company had nearly gone bankrupt and he'd downsized from the big house on Lakeshore. Every day Miss Powers arrived at 9:00 a.m. and stayed until 5:00 p.m. She tried to get Alice to eat grilled-cheese sandwiches or homemade chicken noodle soup. One day she even made brownies. But Alice would not touch any of it. It wasn't that Alice was so in love with Mike that she couldn't function; it had more to do with the fact that he too had disappeared, that their relationship had not been worth much, if anything. It certainly had not been enough to sustain him.

In the beginning of June, Stephanie came to visit and stayed for two nights. Alice didn't have the energy for conversation, so Stephanie alternated between long tête-à-têtes with Alice's father about college football and running out to Northgate Mall. Missy also called several times over the course of the first few weeks, but each time Alice shook her head *no*. Missy sent books on dealing with grief and a chocolate-chip-cookie pie, which Alice's father devoured, even while muttering, "I know I shouldn't, but this is just so darn good . . ."

Everyone assumed that Alice missed Mike, but the real reason she could not move was that his departure had forced her to face a gnawing feeling that something about her wasn't right. Night after night during those last months at school, she'd dragged Mike home and watched him while he slept. Night after night, she'd said nothing to him about his using; instead she'd put him to bed like a small child. She'd *colluded* with him. The truth was, she had not been putting up with him at all; she had relished the role of caretaker. For once, she had felt needed. The more out of control he was, the more in control she felt. When he was like that he could not hurt her; he could not leave her. It was sick to feel that way, and she hated herself for it. What kind of person was she?

For his part, her father was very patient during those first few weeks. He did not try to rouse her from the couch. But on Friday, June 19, a month to the day since she'd returned home, he got up from his chair, sat down on the coffee table, and took Alice's hand. He'd bought her a plane ticket, he said. She would leave on Sunday at noon. If she forced herself to do the internship, he promised things would turn around.

"It's time to get on with life," he said. "It was hard for me to keep going after your mother left, but I did it . . . and now I'm feeling pretty darn good, I have to say."

Later that night, Ziggy called. It was not the first time. Again, she shook her head *no*, but this time her father held the receiver against his chest and whispered, "He's here in Michigan. He's passing through. He wondered if he could stop by tomorrow. I think it would be very rude to say no, don't you?"

The next day Alice's father answered the door. Ziggy held out his hand and said, "Hello, Mr. Townley. I'm Ed Monroe."

Alice, for the first time in a long time, smiled. A genuine smile. Then Missy came through the door, and ran right over to Alice to give her a big hug.

"Oh, honey, I've missed you so much!" she said.

It turned out Ziggy had swung through Boston, where Missy was staying with a friend for the summer, and brought her back home.

Alice's father told them to have a seat on the loveseat across from Alice, then went out to the kitchen to get two Cokes. Missy did most of the talking. She was very animated. Her hands reminded Alice of birds chained around the neck, fluttering up wildly and then flopping back down. She and Ziggy planned to make it to San Francisco by the first, so they'd have plenty of time to stop in the Badlands, a place that Ziggy had always wanted to see. Missy was excited about Yellowstone and Redwood National Park. She wanted to drive through the trees, but neither of them knew whether you were still allowed to do that or whether that was something that only happened back in the olden days.

Alice pushed herself up into a seated position while they talked. She hadn't bothered to shower before they came and suddenly she regretted it. Missy's hair was up in a high ponytail. She was wearing a white dress with tiny cornflowers all over it. A Laura Ashley dress. Innocent. Girlish.

"I wish you'd think about coming with us," Ziggy said.

Missy smiled a tight smile and nodded almost imperceptibly. "Yes," she said. "We do."

"I didn't know I was invited," Alice said.

"Didn't Stephanie ask you when she was here?" Ziggy said, looking over at Missy.

Missy shrugged. "I told her to . . . maybe she thought Alice wasn't up to it."

"Alice is starting her internship in New York on Monday," her father said, returning to the room. He handed Ziggy and Missy their Cokes. "She's going to live with her brother, Raymond."

"I'm sorry Stephanie didn't say anything," Ziggy said. "We could have left earlier. We could have made it out here before your internship. That's why I've been calling you. I've been trying to get in touch for a couple of weeks. Finally I called Missy and she said she needed a ride home anyway. We figured if we both tried, maybe you'd change your mind."

🐎

When Missy and Alice return from the bathroom and sit down again on opposite ends of the white couch, Oscar is reading Stephanie's palm. She's leaning in as if he's an oracle.

"You have lots of money," he says.

"I think you're talking about Alice or Missy," Stephanie says.

"That's a good thing to tell this stranger," Alice says.

"You like sex," Oscar says.

"I used to," Stephanie giggles.

He puts her hand down and takes Missy's. "You have recently been sick," he says.

"That's her," Missy says, pointing at Alice.

He puts down Missy's hand and picks up Alice's. "Your life line, it breaks off and comes back here," he says.

"Good to know," Alice says.

"So, Oscar, tell us about your sex life," Stephanie says.

"What did you have?" Oscar says to Alice. "Should you be smoking like that?"

"I was not physically sick," Alice says, pointing to her head.

Oscar raises his eyebrows.

"She's got problems," Missy says, pointing to her head.

"I know you are sad, but you will find love again," Oscar says to Alice.

Missy makes a clicking sound with her tongue, then picks up her drink. "That has never been her problem," she says.

"What do you want to know?" Oscar picks up Stephanie's hand again. "Ask me anything."

"Tell me something, Oscar," Missy says. "Is it important for you to please a woman?"

"What do you mean by this?" Oscar asks, though it's clear from his little cat-like smile he knows exactly what she means.

"I mean is it enough for you to orgasm or do you want the woman to orgasm too?"

"I'm glad we missed Saba for this," Alice mutters.

"If I don't please her, it will break my heart," Oscar says, looking straight at Alice. "I please her first and then I think of myself."

"See, I told you, Steph," Missy says, with a triumphant smile. "I knew he would say that."

Oscar looks at Alice, probably still hoping to win her over. Suddenly she is filled with rage. She sticks her tongue out at him and he looks away.

"Your friend is very rude," he says to Missy.

"You don't know the half of it," Missy says.

❦

"Please come out with us for a little while," Ziggy said. "We'll be gone in the morning, and who knows when we'll see you again."

"OK," Alice said. "Let me just run to the bathroom first." She got up from the couch, leaving Missy and Ziggy on the loveseat. In the bathroom, she locked the door and sat down on the toilet. She was shaking, so angry with Stephanie and Missy she couldn't breathe. Though she would have said no, it would have been nice if they'd actually had the decency to deliver Ziggy's message. When she got herself under control, she picked up a brush and combed her hair. She changed her clothes and put on deodorant, then walked back out to the living room.

"Let's go," she said, turning to Missy. "You remember The Jungle, that really cool bar downtown? That could be fun."

It was a dance bar with flashing strobe lights that played European techno-pop, songs that went on and on, songs that went right through a person. Alice sat nursing her beer, watching Missy and Ziggy dance. Every time they asked her to join them, she waved them away, until very late when "Every Breath You Take" by the Police came on. Missy was in the bathroom. Ziggy grabbed Alice's hand and yelled, "Come on! This is a great song." On the dance floor, he whispered something in her ear, but she couldn't make out the words. He moved his head away when he was done and smiled. She shook her head, signaling she hadn't caught it. He nodded toward the side door, and she followed him. There was no one else in the alley.

"What did you say in there?" She leaned against the wall.

He moved in closer to her. "I'm in love with you," he said.

"No you aren't, that's ridiculous."

"I knew you'd say that," he said, standing back and running a hand through his hair. "But the thing is, I've been feeling this way for a long time, for a year or more actually. I watched you marching that inebriated ... well, I watched you. I wanted to get to know you. I want you to come with me on this trip. That's why I kept trying to reach you. I called Missy to ask her ... and then she got *all involved*."

Alice didn't know what to say.

"I know you're still upset about Mike, but I just figured this might be my last chance to tell you." The door opened and an older man started through it, but then seeing them, went back inside.

"I don't know what to say," Alice said, looking down. It seemed to her that her legs were like matches, skinny, liable to snap at the slightest touch.

Ziggy fished around until he found the pack of cigarettes in his jacket pocket. He shook one out and handed it to Alice, then lit it for her.

She inhaled deeply. "You don't want to get involved with me," she said. "I'm a terrible person."

Ziggy rolled his eyes. "You're too young to be a terrible person."

"In high school, I ruined someone's life." That was an understatement, but Alice could not manage anymore.

Ziggy laughed and then stopped short when Alice turned away.

"What are you talking about?" he said.

"I did. I got someone in trouble. He got kicked out of school."

"Really? For what?"

"I said he was dealing drugs."

"Why would you do that?"

"In order to save a friend who *was* dealing."

"That is terrible," Ziggy said, and then paused. "But you did it to save a friend. You didn't do the right thing, but your intentions were good."

"I should have gotten Mike help," she said. "I walked him home night after night. I knew how bad it was and I did nothing."

Ziggy shook his head. "Now, that one really wasn't your fault. You couldn't have changed the outcome." He walked over to the ash can next to the door. "Mike had been going off the deep end for a long time and we all saw it. We all tried to stop him. I mean, we all talked to him about it at one point or another."

"You did? I didn't," Alice said. "I wish I had."

"I'm sure he knew that you were trying to help," Ziggy said, with a shrug. "But he didn't want to help himself. There was nothing you could have done about that." He put the pack of cigarettes back in his shirt pocket.

He did look like Keanu Reeves, Alice decided.

"I just wish I could change it. I wish I could change a lot of things."

"I know, but it's over," Ziggy said. "You have to move on. I mean, ruminating? Man! That is a colossal waste of time. You can't let it ruin your whole life."

He had a point. She couldn't change it. Her mother was gone. She'd *left*. Her sister was dead. Her boyfriend was in rehab and wouldn't take her calls—wouldn't see her. Her friends had lied to her. Things just kept happening. There was not one thing she'd actually chosen, not one thing she'd claimed for herself. She didn't have anything. *Nothing*.

"I mean it," Ziggy said. "I don't know why. I know it doesn't make sense. But I really, really dig you."

Alice giggled. He looked so sincere. It was sweet. His eyes were the color of caramels. She grabbed his shirt and kissed him. She was still kissing him when Missy walked through the door.

in the

hermitage

๛

2010

May 3

Dear Alice,

I have been thinking about the fact that I never said good-bye to you—never talked to you after that night senior year. I should have gotten in contact after rehab. I am sorry about that. It wasn't your fault, and you probably still think I blame you.

I'm in Alaska. I'm in a remote location about two hours outside of Anchorage that you cannot reach by car. Igor, the postman, flew me in yesterday. Igor is this old stooped guy of maybe sixty-five, whose right leg is shorter than his left. He moved to Alaska from some remote village in Siberia more than twenty years ago because his wife, Zena, was going crazy out there and now he says (laughingly) she's not feeling much better about life.

He thinks I am crazy to build a cabin out this far, but I told him there aren't many pristine spots left in this world, blah, blah, blah. At one point, he started babbling on about the Lord and how I could use prayer instead of retreating to Alaska, where, next winter, I will probably freeze to death. All that did was remind me that I really dislike jabber jaws and Igor is shaping up to be a big one.

I am not the same fun-loving guy I used to be, Ollie Ollie oxen free.

I know I am probably not going to send these letters to you, but it gives me something to do, and if I were to write to anyone I still think it would be you.

Love,
Mike

May 25

Dear Ollie,

The ice is finally breaking up. Cast out this morning and caught a nineteen-inch trout. Now I've got fish with my beans. I filleted the trout, dunked it in egg, dusted it with cornmeal, and fried it in bacon fat. There is nothing like food cooked over the open fire. I read *Into the Wild* and determined I was not going to be just another guy who dies in a bus. To that end, I am availing myself of a few of the finer things. I mean I have ensured my own survival. I am not as hardcore as McCallister or whatever his name was. I intend to live. I have tools, money, books, liquids, pot. I have Igor to fly the supplies in every couple of weeks—there may be a little more time in between flights come fall, but I will be fully outfitted by then.

I bet you are wondering, why Alaska? I had a friend from my old neighborhood who lived in Anchorage. I flew out here to visit him a few years back and I really dug it. But I didn't want to live in town with him, fishing all summer and drinking all winter. I wanted to live way off the grid. So that's what I'm doing . . .

If I don't get the cabin finished by September 10, I met a guy who is willing to help me. I am not being dumb, is all I'm saying. I do not want to die, exactly.

"We're nothing but brute with a little veneer." I don't know who said it but it's so true. I mean, a lot of the time out here, I'm just thinking about food and where I can find some. It makes me realize that I've never had to worry about that before. Also, I'm thinking about warmth. The first thing I built was a makeshift shed with a tarp for my firewood. I have a sleeping bag that will keep me toasty.

Yesterday, over on the mountain I saw a whole band of Dall sheep. Later, the wind furrowed the lake so that the canoe threatened to roll when I tried to take it out. I parked it and cast off the shore. I could see my breath in the cabin when I woke up and I did not want to get up to feed the stove, but I had to get up and I had to feed that stove. Had a brief panic attack about getting sick or injured and no one finding me for weeks, but that's what the emergency satellite phone is for, I guess. I am easing out of my wussy life. Smoked a bowl just now and am turning in. It's 6:19 p.m. Keeping really weird hours.

Love,
Mike

May 28

Dear Ollie,

I will say one thing. It's not easy to face yourself even when you don't own a mirror. I'm finding that uncomfortable things keep playing over and over in my mind, and I know you know exactly what I am talking about. It's in my mind all the time. It's like a little naked guy crouching in the corner of the room. You can't help seeing him. The room could be really grand. It could be like as big as a football field with gilded mirrors and twenty-foot ceilings, but there's this dude in the corner. Maybe a better visual is someone taking a dump in the corner of the room. I'm high, so all of these metaphors seem enlightened but probably suck.

Fact is, I did some bad shit and every now and then it occurs to me that there are some people who will never escape—I mean they would not have been able to afford to retreat from life. They would not have been able to pay Igor to drop off supplies. They would never even have thought of doing this. And some of them are dead, so it's not an option.

Jesus, I am such an asshole and so are you.

Love,
Mike

June 1

Dear Ollie,

I cheated a little, letting some kids who were at Camp Minton chop down the majority of the spruce logs for the cabin and lay them out for me last August, but I still have to strip them and even them out and drag them back up to my building site, so it's not like I've pawned off the whole job. Last summer I was here just for a couple of weeks camping. Then I purchased the property, which abuts the state forest and Camp Minton, a camp for kids who (I get the impression) have done something wrong and are in Alaska getting their wiring checked. Anyway, they were glad to cut the logs and lay them out for me, and thank God they did, because cutting the grooves, then hauling and stacking, is going to be a big project in and of itself.

My lean-to is about fifty yards from the building site and I do use it most nights because portaging all the way to the cabin is a pain in the ass.

The idea here is to rely on myself. Money is the source of all evil, I believe. I have seen this and you have seen this.

Back in Detroit, every time I mentioned moving to Alaska, people changed the subject. They could not see the point. And that *is* the point. But I don't have anyone to answer to now that Mom and Dad are gone. No one. Yes, they would have been disappointed. Yes, they would have said, "What the fuck?" although not in those words.

Love,
Mike

June 15

Dear Ollie,

It occurred to me that maybe you may not even know what happened to my parents.

My dad died walking into work one day last August. Boom. Down. In the lobby. The next day (and I am not kidding), Rick Hess was promoted to CFO. The network filmed my mom during her cancer treatments. *Can you believe that?* I think that was really the thing, more than anything, that fucked me up. I wonder if you watched it? Seemed like everyone else on the planet did. Her words of wisdom? "Try to make each moment count." Impressive, right? *Pearls of wisdom, Susan.* You should have seen the peace sign from the hospital bed and the shot of her wheeling her IV pole down the hallway and then after she died they did that little memorial on the morning show, but here's the killer (no pun intended): they'd already lined up her replacement, Beth Anne Nichols, the lady with the V-forehead and the bright-green glasses who looks like a housewife doused in Day-Glo.

Excuse me if I don't buy into the whole "make something of yourself" crap.

Love,
Mike

June 22

Dear Ollie,

I have been working too hard on the cabin to write anything the last couple of weeks. I pass out every day at ten at night, when the sun is shining, and I wake up at five thirty in the morning, and it's still shining. I know it goes down around one or two, but I haven't seen it because I am too bushed to stay up that late.

I just read back over these letters. You are not an asshole. I am the asshole. I didn't let you see me in rehab because I was embarrassed. That's it. I wanted to see you, but everyone convinced me that you were a big part of my problem. Using, etc.

The truth is, I am still messed up about Gary and I bet you never let yourself think about it. What happened right after Gary is that you went into one of those fugue states—it was almost like you were really high. I'd see you in the hallway at Fox Grove and you'd walk right by me. You walked right by everyone, looking straight ahead like you were Carrie from that Stephen King movie. It was bizarre, but what could you have done? You knew it was your fault he got expelled but you couldn't say it, could you? And I am *at fault*. I talked you into it. I told you to frame him. I didn't want to get caught for dealing and I wanted you to pin it on him and you did. I think maybe you really did love me. We never said it, did we? *What a shame*, as my mother used to say when she was interviewing people.

Coiled. That's how I would describe you if questioned by the authorities.

Now that I've written all of this, I am sure I will never send these letters to you and that is a shame because we should have had a heart-to-heart.

At least once.

Anyway, I am sorry I wouldn't see you when you called, but I didn't want you to see me like that. I was in North Wing II. Holbrook scared the fuck out of me. Twenty-one years old and I've got a big greasy guy named Ray strip-searching me. Metal detectors, no knives, no pencils, no nothing. They even took away my Clearasil. Not sure if they thought I was going to eat it or what. Old people, young people. Everyone fucked up. The whole thing sucked, but let's not dwell on sad things. All of this is ancient history. Decades have passed. I don't know why I'm riding these emotional waves. It's very intense out here.

Since I've been here I've planted rhubarb, potatoes, peas, carrots, and beets. Beets only because Igor's wife, Zena, sent me some starter plants. I'm not really a fan of beets.

Random thought: I had this crazy nanny named Maureen— this was before you knew me, before we moved to Detroit. Woman was seriously nuts. I didn't eat these beets she made, so she literally poured them out on the floor and made me pick them up and then eat them. I sat at the table for five hours. When I tried to get up, she hit me with a spatula.

Two weeks ago, I planted fifteen hills of potatoes. So far I've laid and notched thirty-eight logs and set the base with gravel. The place is going to be big enough for a bunk bed, a desk, shelves, a pot-bellied stove, a fireplace, and two windows, one overlooking the lake. I'm almost ready for the eave logs. It's been ten days since I cut the first notch. Not bad. If I keep this up, I'll be able to move in by August.

I would love it if you came to see me, but how would you get here? And why would you ever want to come? I heard about Ziggy. Hooking up with (and then marrying!) my fraternity brother—so not cool. Not cool at all. I didn't find out for almost a year because nobody wanted to jeopardize my "sobriety."

I remember nights when we'd smoked and we were sprawled out on your couch and you'd pass out and I'd watch you. Sometimes I'd run a finger up the inside of your arm just to feel how smooth the skin was there. We were as close as two fucked-up teenagers could be, but we both had those walls. The way your shoulders hunched or you flinched. The way you clammed up around Steve Davis or Matt Edwards. You always seemed like you were trying to escape notice.

When I picture you in my mind's eye I see you staring out a window at the snow like some forlorn woman in a nineteenth-century novel.

Maybe it wasn't just love—maybe it was also pity . . . mixed with a tiny bit of lust.

More than a tiny bit, possibly.

Love,
Mike

June 30

Dear Ollie,

I'd love to see some of our friends' faces right now . . . They would never believe where the Dustman ended up.

I have been haunted the last few nights and perhaps it was brought on by the bug bites. I have to tell Igor to bring DEET next time he comes. I have been literally ripping my skin off. I keep thinking about my mom and some of the crazy shit that went down before she died. How she didn't want to face it. She was only fifty-five, so I guess she felt like it wasn't her time and she was so successful . . . But it was not the end that got me . . . it was all the months leading up to it, how she kept putting on that happy face and telling everyone it was going to be all right. People would say, "You ought to clean out your drawers," "You should get your will in order," and she refused to do it. She didn't even dump her vibrator. I found it rolled up in a towel in the back of her closet under her Chanel purse collection. I mean, she knew she was dying, so what the fuck was she thinking?

I had to clean everything out of the basement. I found a picture of my grandmother and my first dog, Red, which I brought with me and have hanging by what is still just a window hole. My grandmother saved my life. If she hadn't taken me in every summer vacation when I was little, I would have ended up wandering the streets with these effed-up kids in my old neighborhood . . . this is before you knew me. One of the kids had a mother who was loony tunes—she used to march around in circles singing show tunes. Then she offed herself. All her son ever did was cry. It was pathetic—or at least that's what I thought then. Now I think, good for him being able to cry.

My grandmother had this next-door neighbor, this old guy named Ralph, who fought in World War II. Ralph and his wife were my best friends when I was a little kid. Their son was gone and they were lonely, so they baked cookies with me and took me to the zoo and the ice-cream store. My grandmother was a caretaker, so she was busy. I loved that old guy. One of the last times I saw him I was like sixteen or seventeen and pretty fucked-up. I mean I was a total prick. I could tell he was sad about it. I was a disappointment. Then at the end of that summer, he moved down to see his son and a couple of years later my grandmother told me he passed away. The thing I keep remembering is that last summer he would run out into the street in the middle of the night, screaming and crying. He was sure he was still in the Pacific under attack by the Japs. Freaky. I guess he was losing it. It is so hard to recover from things. The war had ended more than forty years before, but he was still fighting in it.

If I do that up here, I'm a goner—I mean run outside. Especially in the winter. I wonder if the cold would jolt me awake?

Love,
Mike

July 6

Dear Ollie,

The rutabaga is coming up. Not sure what I'm going to do with it. I cut a hole in the earth and put a Tupperware container in so I have a cooler. I have some butter in there and four-dozen eggs.

Today, I secured the roof poles over the gables. Mosquitos, no-see-ums, black flies—all are still an issue. I was trying to read out on this little strip of gravel next to the water—I call it my mini-beach—and all these bugs were making a regular happy meal out of me. I haven't mentioned it, but I brought *Moby Dick* up here and figured that will keep me busy for at least a year. This is part of the lesson of living here, Ollie—sticking with things, seeing them through. The longer the book, the better. A man looks into the abyss and all that.

The other thing I have to do is think about the money and what to do with it. My parents' money. The question is whether to give it away. I have to have some money in case of an emergency, but how much is enough? Will I be here for the rest of my life? Will I really be able to function without a cushion? Every time Igor brings me supplies it costs me, but if I stay here my expenses won't be more than twenty or thirty grand a year even with flying out for holidays, etc. If I ever even do that. I have a feeling I might start to go mad at some point and then I might really need some extra cash. Isn't it interesting that every time I convince myself to do something nice, something altruistic, I talk myself right out of it?

Love,
Mike

July 12

Dear Ollie,

So Gary jumped off the MacArthur Bridge into the Detroit River, and he was unconscious when he was recovered by that twenty-five-foot small boat from Station Belle Isle. They did CPR and he was revived. They transferred him to Detroit Receiving Hospital.

Now that is one hell of a serious story, but despite all of that information, you and I joked about him just being high and losing his footing. Remember that? We had a second chance to save him, but we still didn't do anything. We could have gone straight to Principal Altman and told him that we framed Gary, but even *after he jumped into the fucking river*, we didn't do it.

I didn't think about Gary again until I was out of rehab and working in New York. I ran into Somers (remember her—a year younger than us?) and she said that after we graduated there was a big brouhaha at Fox Grove—protesters out front, etc.—because people were upset about what happened to Gary. I guess he was really bright and it was a big deal that he won that scholarship. For some reason that was when it finally hit me. I started *thinking*. And I mean *thinking* about it. I started wondering where he was and what he was doing. After I graduated I did a little investigating and discovered he was working as a security guard at the Detroit Institute of Arts, so I told myself he had a nice job in an art museum and I told myself that was not so bad. Yes, we did something wrong, but in the end everything worked out. And I let it go.

Love,
Mike

July 30

Dear Ollie,

Saw caribou cows and calves on the hillside this morning. Need to start stuffing the oakum between the logs, but I was so hungry I took the fly rod down to the lake and cast out. The minute I did, a salmon hit. Seventeen and one-fourth inches long. I was so hungry, I almost ran back to the cabin with it. Left the entrails on the beach for the magpies and that's when I saw the brown bear and the cub. This huge brown bear was just sprawled out on her back with her paws in the air and the cub was suckling. At first I really thought the mama was dead; she had her face turned to the side and a slight smile. Who knew bears had so many tits? They were large and black and I was pretty far away but there might have been like four of five. I kept inching forward, trying to get a better look (sounds kinky, I know), and then she opened one eye and saw me. She leapt up and started barreling right toward me. Luckily, I was only about twenty yards away from the cabin and I have the door up now, but the roof isn't done, so I just hunkered down praying she wouldn't climb through the rafters. Have to ask Igor what the story is . . . I don't think it's a great thing when a bear is hanging around your front door.

Love,
Mike

August 2

Dear Ollie,

A wolf killed a caribou last night. Peeled his skin off easy as an apple rind. I was watching from the cabin window, which luckily I have glass for now as Igor dropped it off yesterday. This made me realize that some animals just kill other animals. That's what they do. And the stronger ones survive. Period. The world is an inhospitable place for a thinking man.

Insects remain a huge aggravation despite the DEET. Saw a spider the size of my hand in the wood shavings yesterday, so I spent the rest of the day sweeping down the entire cabin and shining my flashlight into every corner.

Igor says I am going to have to kill that mama bear and the cub. He says that once a bear discovers your camp, then it's either you or her and I was lucky (according to Igor) that she left without breaking down the door that day. He says normally a bear won't give up. I have two shotguns and I keep them fully loaded. I am the most paranoid person on the planet right about now. If you saw me walking around here, you would laugh your ass off.

Last night I woke up twice dreaming about Gary. I don't know why now, all of a sudden, but I suppose it's because there's nothing else going on. Sometimes, the noise inside my ears is deafening. Like a ringing sound. You'd be surprised how annoying it can get. I spent half of yesterday with my head buried under my pillow, trying to unhear it. But I couldn't get it to stop and then when I went outside all I could hear were the shorebirds or seagulls or what have you screeching, "Why, why, why?" and the water was all riled up and the waves made these echoing sounds that reminded me of people slamming their lockers in high school. Remember the way that echoed? I am not sure I am going to be able to handle this isolation all winter.

Mike

August 12

Dear Ollie,

Put the tar paper down on the roof and the polyethylene over it. Some old guy wandered up named Mike Mushroom. I kid you not. I tried very hard not to laugh when he introduced himself and it took everything out of me. Mike Mushroom is close to seven-feet tall, and he's got a thick gray beard and hair that sits on the top of his head like a giant tumbleweed. He said his cabin is just a mile off and he's been living here since the sixties, but he leaves in September every year and returns on the first of May. He even knew Dick P., who is a famous hermit around "these here parts." I don't know how Mike Mushroom found my cabin and I don't know how or when he departed. We smoked a bowl. He told me that I shouldn't stay the winter, then he took off (I thought he was just taking a leak), and I can't find one trace of him anywhere. Not even a footprint. Later, I went kind of nuts for a little while thinking I imagined him and he was really just me twenty years from now if I stay here. My perceptions are a little dicey sometimes in "these here parts."

Mike

August 15

Dear Ollie,

Cut the moss for the roof into eighteen-by-thirty-six-inch squares. Must have cut a couple of acres of moss and still didn't have enough for the whole roof. I am running late as it can start snowing in September.

Jack dropped off some eggs, milk, butter, bread, flour, rice, sugar, cornmeal, an extra sleeping bag, and a canning kit. I asked him about Mike Mushroom and he looked at me like I was insane. He said, "If there is a guy named Mike Mushroom, I have never heard of him, and I don't miss much." That scared me a little. Then he took it back—he said that there are people who are completely off his radar and everyone else's. It can happen.

Igor stayed an hour or so. Showed me how his wife makes blueberry jam and cranberry sauce. I have twenty-four jars and a shelf in the cabin to store my delicacies, provided I can figure out how to make preserves. There's a lot more work here than I expected. I mean, just fishing, cutting logs, hauling water, and hunting takes up all my time. I need to have at least four full cords to keep warm this winter and that is a crazy amount.

Mike

August 20

Dear Ollie,

Hung the door. Went blueberry picking up on the pass and then caught a lake trout for dinner. Now the birds know I'm going to leave the entrails and they crowd around me. It's pretty cool. Saw the bear again last night but she was a ways off so I didn't take a shot. I'd almost forgotten about her. It's the first time I've seen her in a couple of weeks.

Love,
Mike

September 3

Dear Ollie,

Building the fireplace was not something I felt like I could do alone, so last week Igor brought in two masons from Anchorage. They stayed a week and helped me haul up the sand from the lake and work the cement. We had to cut through the logs and fashion the arch. You would not believe how many rocks we had to bring up from the lake. The arch is six inches thick. Just as we were finishing up, the mortar and beach gravel were starting to freeze up overnight. The guys, whose names are Tiny (he's not) and Sam, have been camping out on the bluff behind the cabin. They think I'm nuts to stay the winter, but if I insist on it, they think I should get a dog to keep me company. I told them I don't want to be responsible for anyone else out here. Tiny said, "Dog wouldn't expect much from you." *Not much is still something*, I thought, but I didn't say it. They also said a dog would warn me if the bear came back again, which they assured me she would—especially as it's getting colder.

They were happy with what I paid them. I asked them what they do in the city during the winter when it's dark and they don't have much work and they said they spend a lot of time at the bar or playing chess by the fire. Doesn't that sound nice? I think I would be better off if I had some neighbors. This may have been a miscalculation on my part.

Love,
Mike

October 5

Dear Ollie,

Two feet of snow on the ground and I am busy nonstop just keeping the path cleared down to the lake. Tried to set a beaver trap but I lost part of it beneath the ice. I have amassed a huge cache in the cabin. Lots of preserves and eggs and evaporated milk, sugar, flour, cornmeal. Just on my own rations, I could survive the winter, I think. I am getting really lazy though. This is one thing you absolutely cannot be out here and it's the one thing I most definitively am—lazy. I use a lot of wood every day . . . more than I anticipated. And here's another bummer: My hands freeze up faster than they should. It's almost like something's wrong with me. I can't be out there for more than five minutes and my hands are frozen stiff. Igor is bringing me some better gloves and some of those things you can stick in them that heat up. I am glad I cut so much firewood last August. I could never have handled it now. I know I'm just being a baby. Sometimes I wake up at night and the wind is whistling and I think it's people laughing at me: you, my mom, my dad, some of the kids at school.

I wrote a letter to my aunt Krissie asking her to look up Gary's family on the Internet. See if she can find them. I want to give them something, Ollie, even if it doesn't change anything. Honestly, I wish I had an Internet connection here. It's hard to take.

I have dreams about my mom and then I become convinced that she's haunting me, which would be pretty unlikely considering she never paid any attention to me when she was actually alive. You know the worst thing about it? I don't resent her for having her career and being so involved and not being around. I don't resent my dad either, but what really bothers me is that I wasn't able to feel anything when they died. I felt numb. Even though my mom apologized at the end for never being around. She even cried. It was almost like I was watching a movie. (Well, we were being filmed by her TV show, so . . .) I just sat there in the chair next to her bed and stared down at her. I kept saying it was all right and I didn't hold it against her and what else could she do? I told her what she wanted to hear and I think it helped her. But I didn't *feel* anything. Not a thing. You're the only person I've ever cared about even a little bit . . . you and maybe that old guy Ralph. Isn't that sad? The only time I feel like crying is when I think about that pathetic fact. Something tells me you know exactly what I'm talking about.

Love,
Mike

November 28

Dear Ollie,

Thanksgiving Day. Big rams up on the side of the mountain with full curls. I made a feast—hotcakes and cranberry sauce, turnips, small red potatoes, beets.

OK, I told you the first part about Gary but I neglected to tell you the ending.

Fast-forward.

I didn't get another update on Gary until last year right before I moved here. I drove down to the DIA and started wandering around. I went into that portrait gallery on the second floor and it was empty except for a guard standing by the door, so I walked up to him and asked him if he knew Gary. He said sure, Gary had worked there for fifteen years. He was always talking about college and how he was saving up for college, but then he got some girl pregnant, so instead of going to college, he got married. Now he has six kids, which is tough I'm sure on a security guard's salary. The guy said he had worked his way up to floor supervisor and was doing well.

It doesn't totally suck, but it's not rocket science.

Love,
Mike

December 1

Dear Ollie,

This is alternately great and terrible. It reminds me of this one time I went hiking in Yellowstone. I was fifteen. My parents took me to Yellowstone and then they sent me around on all of these different tours by myself while they looked at "property." Anyway, one day I decided to hike up to Angel Falls by myself. I was in terrible shape as you might recall and I kept passing people on the way up to the falls who said things like "You're almost there," "You're probably three-fourths of the way," etc., etc., but it was so hot and I didn't have anything to drink and I kept thinking, "There is no way I am ever going to get there." Once I got there I knew I had to hike all the way back. That's how this feels on a much grander scale. I mean there is no way out now because two to four weeks goes by between drops (Igor) and I just have to sit this one out. I wish I'd brought more to read than *Moby Dick* and I'm going to have to ask Igor to bring some alternatives next time because believe it or not—I finished it last week.

Love,
Mike

December 5

Dear Ollie,

Weirdest thing ever—I was lying in the cabin just looking at the wall yesterday (I admit it—I was under the covers midday just staring at the wall) when someone knocked on my door. It scared the shit out of me! Turned out it was Mike Mushroom. He came in and sat down and we smoked a bowl. He said he decided to stay the winter after all. When I asked him why he said, "Every few years I do it to toughen myself up again." He looks plenty tough to me. In fact, a little scary knowing that I'm out here with a guy like Mike Mushroom and nobody else around for hundreds of miles. I asked him if he was well stocked for the winter and he said he probably has enough meat stored in his homemade freezer (dug into the permafrost—quite a feat) to last a couple of years. Berries were light this summer so he might run out of jam/syrup, but otherwise he's good. I might have imagined it, but I thought I saw him looking at my cache a little greedily . . . I probably am paranoid.

He did the same thing again—went out for a leak and just disappeared.

Love,
Mike

December 13

Dear Ollie,

Going out for wood and then I think I'll spend the rest of the day in bed rereading *Moby Dick*.

It has been eight days since Mike Mushroom visited last and I'm so lonely I think I'd even enjoy a visit from the crazy man himself.

Love,
Mike

in the

museum

of your life

2011

A lice's children were almost grown. In Detroit, where once
there had been run-down buildings and garbage heaps,
prairie grass now prevailed. Despite evidence to the contrary,
Alice's husband Ed remained convinced the city was poised for
a comeback.

Lately, with college looming, he had pressed her to make a
comeback too. The problem was that Alice had no marketable skills.
She had not left the suburbs in almost two decades. When she'd
last worked, commuters listened to Walkman stereos and the news
came into the office over the wire. She'd been a journalist, and for
all intents there were no journalists anymore. There were women
who appeared to stride the line between hooker and newsreader,
young and unabashedly flaunting their silicone-enhanced breasts

in tight-fitting shirts. Journalists with less substantial physical attributes seemed to post their stories on the Internet. They wrote about whatever moved them, free from both constraint and compensation.

Getting a job she qualified for would not be lucrative—it might not even be feasible. In lieu of a better plan, Alice took to driving. If she got in the car and headed east or west or north or south, at some point she would end up somewhere and it felt more proactive than waiting for destiny to knock on the front door like a Jehovah's Witness. It was refreshing not to have to *be* anywhere in particular. Two decades of motherhood had made her appreciative of her free time.

One day, she navigated her SUV toward the city. Her house, twenty minutes from the city, was far enough away that she hardly ever went downtown. In front of city hall, people were picketing. The signs indicated that the automobile company they worked for had relocated to Mexico. Now these leftover people were standing outside on a frigid January day wielding homemade signs. Alice wondered whether anyone who was in a position to address their concerns was still residing in the USA. In the old days when she was a reporter, she would have gotten out of the car and asked some questions. Now that she was older, she felt like she already knew more about most things than she wanted to.

She was about to turn back toward home when she remembered the art museum and changed her mind. In front of the art building was a copy of Rodin's famous sculpture *The Thinker*. She slowed down to look at him. He had been sitting there longer than she'd been alive, and he still hadn't figured anything out.

Inside the museum, there was no one but a little old lady with a pink bow and a cat sweater sitting behind a card table. She wanted to know whether Alice would like to pay seventy-five dollars for a yearly membership.

"No," Alice said. "I'm just visiting this once."

"It's pretty self-explanatory," the woman said, handing her a map.

Alice took the map and headed down the hall. When they were first married, she and Ed had spent a lot of time in this museum, but when the children were little they gave it up because, according to Ed, there was nothing worse than traipsing through a place you once revered for art and solemnity with screaming children, who out of boredom were liable to knock into a sculpture or throw a fit in the middle of the marble hallway.

On the first floor, she wandered with a feeling of vague panic through the Egyptians, the Native Americans, and the Asian and Islamic cultures. There was so much she didn't know. What was she looking at? A carved wooden piece called *Reclining Figure* appeared to be a depiction of a man canoodling with a snake. A round wooden bowl meant to be a ravenous Sioux spirit looked like a cartoon character with two eyes perched on a stomach. All these vessels, utensils, urns, statues. All of the ancient gods. How did all of these items end up in this room so far removed from the people who once used them?

The British—especially the men—were big fans of portraits. Portraits, portraits, portraits. Everyone seemed to be staring disapprovingly out at Alice. Rembrandt Peale, the same man who had painted a large canvas of death on the second floor, had painted many self-portraits up on the third. Two hung on the wall side by side. In one picture he was young, and in the other he was thirty years older. Did he think he still looked good, or was he painting it in spite of the ravages of time? He looked so proud of himself in the older picture. The same could not be said of many women she knew. It would not occur to a middle-aged woman to paint of self-portrait. Come to think of it, it would not occur to many young women either.

A throng of high schoolers charged through the gallery in green plaid skirts and navy-blue pants. Alice checked the logo on a redhead's shirt to see if they were students from her alma mater but they were not. The teenagers looked either stone-cold detached or agitated, hyper, irreverent; either way they paid no attention to their surroundings. Their guide, an old man with a black, beanie-sized beret and a permanent sneer, pointed to the paintings, but the students refused to humor him. The teacher, a tight-lipped elderly woman with hair as matted and wet-looking as papier-mâché, hissed, "Stop giggling," "Stop fooling around," "Look at the artwork!"

Alice sat down on a cushioned bench in the middle of the room and turned away from the kids. Maybe if she concentrated she would be able to learn something from the guide. She'd been on a zillion field trips like the one she was now witnessing and she'd never retained one teaspoonful of information—not in the science museum, not at the zoo, not in the ice-cream store in her suburb where the owner had demonstrated how to make mint chocolate chip. When she emerged from the school bus after those long field trips, she always felt like she'd been run through a blender.

As she waited for the guide to continue, she looked up at the paintings in front of her and a sensation went through her, a shock like touching an unexpectedly hot surface: it was a painting of a young man with white-blond hair wearing a shirt with a tall standing collar and a dark vest and overcoat. She got up and checked the card next to the painting. She had never heard of the artist; the painting had been commissioned in 1832, but the man in it looked exactly like Mike, her best friend, her first love, who had moved to Alaska and had never returned. Apparently he'd tried to walk back to civilization after his cabin burned to the ground the previous winter. The only thing they found, months later, were his hiking boots about a mile and a half from the cabin. Alice hadn't seen or heard from Mike in years, but when a friend had shared the news of his disappearance (learned like so much these days on Facebook) she had been devastated, was still broken up about it. She wished she could have talked to him one last time. So many things she should have said.

This portrait even had the same pouting lips, blond hair, and pale complexion as Mike. A spot of white paint in the eyes made it look like he was holding back tears. The lips were wet like Mike's often were with beer or scotch or whatever liquor was on hand—he'd never been picky. The man in the painting was looking off to the right. She moved to the side as if to catch his eye.

When Alice turned around she realized that even the security guard had disappeared into an adjacent gallery. She was alone with the people on the wall. She sat down to spend more time staring back at Mike. If only he were here, what would he make of her life? Boring. That's what.

At lunchtime, Alice purchased a salad in the cafeteria and picked out a table in the middle of the atrium right underneath the glass dome. Once she was sitting, she pulled out her book, *Life After Life*, and started to read. The book was about a woman who got to repeat her life over and over. Although she didn't realize she was living the same life multiple times, with each successive run-through she made better choices because she would get a feeling of déjà vu and correct her past mistakes. It was the best book Alice had read in a long time. If Alice had to do it over again, she would still have married Ed, who made her laugh, but she would not have stayed in this location. She would have moved somewhere warm and sunny. She would have changed almost everything about her childhood. In the book, *Life After Life*, the heroine gets to go back and save several people's lives—family members, friends, acquaintances. Most deaths, it turned out, were just a matter of closing a door or saying "no" to an outing instead of "yes." Sometimes you could prevent a death just by putting down the phone.

When Alice looked up from her book, she realized that every person in the room qualified for the senior discount, except for a couple at the next table who looked to be around Alice's age. The woman had black hair cut fashionably so that the ends framed her face like fingers. She wore yoga pants and a sweatshirt, and Alice guessed she too had just driven down from the suburbs for lunch. The husband or boyfriend was wearing a gray suit and might have just emerged from a bank or a law firm. They were leaning into one another, talking. Their animated expressions fascinated Alice. She bent her head and pretended to read, so they wouldn't realize she was listening to every word.

"Can you believe we didn't even know?" the woman said.

"Well, who would have guessed *that*?"

"A Nazi!"

"She wasn't a Nazi. She said she didn't even know what Hitler was up to," the wife said.

"Give me a break! How could she not have known?"

"I don't know, but I believed her until that day I had Tina over? I think it was her curly hair. Afterward Bettina said, 'Is your friend Jewish?' and just the way she said the word *Jewish* . . . that was it for me. She must be like ninety-five now. Martha told me she's still alive. She lives alone."

"We dropped her like a bad habit."

"That's one for the books though . . . our Nazi babysitter."

"How can she even function on a daily basis?" the husband said. "Either she knew and did nothing or she didn't know but—"

Alice couldn't hear the end of his sentence because the man got up from the table, his chair scraping. She watched him lope over to the condiments bar. What was he going to say? Alice thought about turning to ask the woman but she didn't have the nerve.

The next week Alice returned to the museum. She had mentioned her initial visit to Ed, and to his credit he did not suggest that if she had time to wander around museums she could have set aside a few minutes to sort his socks. That was the response she had expected. Instead he'd said, "I should go back sometime myself," but then he'd opened the newspaper and stuck his head in it and Alice didn't go the further step of inviting him along.

The truth was Ed had transformed from a poet—the most romantic man she'd ever met—to a killjoy who only cared about golf and checking the stock market. It had to do with kids and raising them and providing for them, and these things were admirable, Alice could see that. But at night when they sat together and debated TV selections, she wondered when they'd decided it was OK to watch these screen people in lieu of living. She was now a middle-aged woman who was glued to the television every night and roamed the city liked a specter during the day. Perhaps that was what happened to everyone. You started out feeling that anything was possible and then life got in the way. That sounded like something she might read on a billboard. It was more than that, wasn't it? You started out. You made decisions. They seemed to be decisions that you could go back on, that you could do over, but then one day you realized you'd made too many choices. There was no way to retract them. Ed had chosen to make money. Maybe that came from living among people who valued money. That decision had cost him his dream. Now when she brought up the fact that life was going by fast and that they needed to make a change, they needed to map out the next stage or it would pass them by, he acted like frittering one's life away on the golf course wasn't such a bad thing.

The little old woman was sitting at the card table again. This time she was wearing an orange bow and a pumpkin sweater. "I will buy a membership," Alice said.

"Great!" the woman muttered as she extracted a membership form from the top right-hand drawer of her tiny desk. How many people actually came back, and what could be said about the sorry folk who did?

The longer Alice looked, the more the paintings seemed to resemble people she'd once known. Rembrandt Peale looked like the father of her high-school friend, Missy. Missy's father had been a philanderer, and his second wife, an aesthetician, was as fluffy and ornamented as his first wife was plain and thin. He'd screwed them both over in the end. The last Alice heard he was living in Aruba with a Pilates instructor. Aside from brief reunions instigated by other friends, she never saw Missy anymore because Missy still acted like she was in high school—as if anyone cared whether a woman nearing fifty sported pearl-white teeth or could still wear a size two. Alice was not contemptuous of her middle-aged friends who worked out maniacally or acquired sports cars, but she couldn't understand why they thought those things would ever compensate for other, more substantial losses.

Sisters on the Shore was on the second level, in the back near the restrooms, and when Alice asked the portly guard standing in the doorway, he said it had been hanging there for years.

"But I've been in here before and never seen it," Alice said.

The guard shrugged. He said he'd been working at the DIA for thirty years and it hadn't moved an inch.

It was a painting of two little girls at the seashore, the older one standing with her arm protectively draped over her little sister. Alice almost never thought about Queenie's death. Her parents traveled so much when she was growing up, because they couldn't bear to spend time in town—"all the pitying looks," her mother used to say. They went to great lengths to avoid Ridge Road, the thoroughfare in the middle of town where it had happened. Alice sometimes still suffered a gnawing, empty feeling when she thought of Queenie; the only clear memory she had was playing in their fort together and the sound of Queenie's voice when she was whining, how annoying that had been and how she missed it after she was gone. For a year afterward Alice had dragged her blanket into the bathroom and slept in the bathtub because she was afraid to be in her big bedroom alone. She'd always shared a room with Queenie and couldn't stand to see her empty twin bed. Finally, she asked her mother to get rid of the other bed, and her mother did.

Alice took the stairs up to European Art. The first painting she encountered was a large cathedral whose Gothic spires resembled Fox Grove, her former high school. How beautiful her high school had been, how lucky she was to attend, and how little she'd appreciated it. Instead she'd spent the entire four years getting in trouble with Mike.

Alice returned to the portrait gallery for another look at Mike. It was kind of sad, wanting to go back and see him again, and Alice wondered if this was the beginning of the end, if when she got older she would start associating every movie, book, or piece of artwork with events from her own life and people she had known. Perhaps that was what older people did with their time. They sat on park benches and in cafés and wandered museums, every encounter floating free of time and space happening now and happening again.

The gallery was filled with more school children. Another private school. This group also sported the same requisite khakis and navy shirts. An African American boy, tall and thin as a light pole, walked toward the portrait on the wall that looked like Mike. Alice checked his logo, which said "Markham," not "Fox

Grove." She didn't recognize the name. When she asked where the school was, he said that it was a new private school on the west side.

"But I live just down the street from the museum," he added. "I commute to school."

"You like coming here?" she said.

He had been studying the painting and making notes in a booklet.

"Sure, I grew up coming here all the time," he said. "My dad used to be a security guard here."

"He doesn't work here anymore?"

"He quit. Now he's back in school. He wants to be an aerospace engineer."

"Awesome," Alice said.

The boy nodded.

"That guy looks like a friend of my dad's," the kid said, pointing to the Mike look-alike.

"I was just thinking he looks like my old boyfriend," Alice said.

At that moment, the teacher poked her head back into the gallery. "Thomas, time to get going."

The security guard was staring at Alice. He was a large, pink-faced man with gold spectacles and broken blood vessels crisscrossing his cheeks and nose. He looked like he should have been a butcher or a construction worker. His forearms, crossed in front of his chest, were beefy. A flap of his forehead hung down like a shelf above his eyes, which made him look like he was scowling.

Alice walked over to him. "Are most of your visitors school children?" she said.

"Pretty much," he said, without uncrossing his arms or smiling. "That and retirees like myself."

"How long have you been doing this?" Alice said.

"Since I left the force last year," he said. "DPD."

The guard's walkie-talkie squawked. A voice came through, but Alice could not understand it. The guard muttered something in response and turned to Alice. "They want me down in Islamic."

Alice watched him walk away toward the exit.

"What were you talking to that guard about?" A voice sounded out behind Alice and she jumped. It was Ed. He was holding a brown bag. With his gray hair, in his charcoal-gray business suit, he looked a little like her own father but thinner. She noticed he held a small spiral notepad with a red cover in his other hand.

"Nothing," Alice said. "What's that for?" She pointed to his brown bag.

"I thought I'd give it a try, coming at lunch, knocking out a poem or two."

"Good idea."

Alice asked Ed about his day and received the usual response that it had been fine. In the American gallery they paused in front of Whistler's *Nocturne in Black and Gold, The Falling Rocket*.

"This one just looks like a bunch of sparklers raining down," Ed said.

"Yeah, but what are those?" Alice said, pointing to the bottom of the painting. "Those look like ghosts on the beach."

"They do. It's kind of a dismal-looking celebration if that's what it's supposed to be," Ed said.

"I can't tell if it's a celebration like July Fourth or a plane crash."

"Me neither," Ed said. "Are you hungry?"

Alice said she was, even though she wasn't.

In the cafeteria, Alice took a tray and Ed went to get a seat. She studied all of the selections but nothing looked enticing. She slid her tray past the macaroni and cheese and the grilled chicken, then went out to the seating area. Ed was sitting in the back by a large ficus. He waved to her and she started past the other diners toward him.

"So are you going to try to write again?" Alice said, when they were seated.

"Maybe," Ed shrugged. "I miss the creative outlet. It's been years since we had any free time."

"True," Alice said.

They ate in silence for a minute.

"Do you ever regret moving here?" Alice said.

"Not really," Ed said. "I think everything worked out pretty well."

"You do?" Alice emptied a sugar into her coffee.

"Yeah, I mean, I was never going to be Walt Whitman. If I had that kind of talent, maybe I would be disappointed. But I don't think I could be any better off, personally. I love my wife, I love my kids. I have a good job."

"What about the city?"

"What about it?"

"It's depressing," Alice said. "Sometimes when I'm driving around down here I just want to cry. It's like always being on the verge of death, you know? It's like constantly being reminded that Kevorkian has the machine all set up for you."

Ed laughed. "I have no idea what you mean by that."

"If we lived somewhere else we could pretend like the world is a good place and everything works out. But here you can't pretend." Alice smacked her hand against her head. "I mean, it's right in your face all the fucking time."

"I don't know that that's a bad thing," Ed said.

"It might not be a bad thing." Alice took a sip of her coffee. "But it still sucks."

"It sucks worse for the people who are living it," Ed said.

Later, outside, the sky was bright and the day stretched out before her. Ed turned to walk back to the office. He said that they should meet at the DIA again, that he'd enjoyed it, and she agreed. He waved good-bye without asking where she was heading, which was good because she didn't know.

garden

for the

blind

2014

Despite all of her warnings to her daughter Denise, Alice was being escorted into the principal's office again, the sixth time in the past two years. To make matters worse, Principal Barich was engaged in a heated telephone conversation when she arrived. He signaled for Alice to have a seat, then rotated his swivel chair toward the window and continued shouting in German into the phone.

Alice sat down in the armchair across from the desk. Ed had not returned her call. She knew she shouldn't even be surprised. He was embroiled in a meeting on increased turmoil in the U.S. trade markets; if this kept up then the company would definitely go under for good. Plus they were under fire from the union, as usual. Lots of press. She hadn't expected him to come running, but how was it that he was incapable of ignoring six desperate phone calls? If he'd noted her repeated attempts to reach him, the least he could have done was call back. Alice was concerned that Denise had pushed Principal Barich too far this time. Without her husband's cache, she might be powerless.

Principal Barich slammed the phone down.

"I'm sorry," he said, with a tight smile. "My sister in Wegberg." Then, with no preamble, he detailed Denise's latest infractions. She and her boyfriend, along with several others, had been caught with pot in their lockers *again*.

Mr. Barich sighed. "All of the students involved in this fiasco have been suspended for two weeks. Furthermore, I've decided they will all—especially Denise—spend that time giving back. For the next week, each student will perform community service at different locations all over the city. As for Denise, just this morning, right before all of this took place, I received a call from the Mt. Carmel School for the Blind in Detroit. They're looking for volunteers to help plant a new garden for their students. Denise will work at the School for the Blind every day from eight in the morning until the regular school day ends at three thirty."

"In Detroit?" Alice said.

"I know it's a little rough in spots." When Principal Barich looked up, Alice could have sworn there was a gleam in his eye. "But the principal assured me that the garden is secured on three sides by a stone wall and in the front by six-foot wrought iron gates that they keep locked at all times."

Principal Barich flicked through a drawer and withdrew a Xerox copy of a newspaper article.

"I pulled this up on the web," he said, handing it to Alice.

Garden Delights Blind Students

Teacher Mary Whelan was inspired by the teachings of Rosemary Kenney, a renowned horticultural therapist, when she decided that auditory and tactile stimulation in the form of a garden might help her blind students better navigate through the world at large. "When one door closes," Mrs. Whelan said, "another one opens." The garden is in need of volunteers before opening day on June 15. Come see the world through our eyes!

"This is total bullshit!" Denise said when Alice told her. They had not said a word the whole way home until Alice pulled into the driveway and announced that she would wake Denise up at seven the following morning.

"No way, I'm going to get some zees this week," Denise said, swiping at her long bangs. She did this constantly because she refused to pin them back or wear a headband. Her hair looked like a woven mat hanging down in front of her eyes.

"No sleep this week," Alice said, handing her the article. "I consider this your last chance, young lady."

"This is bullshit," Denise repeated, kicking the door shut.

Watching Denise, with her scraggly jeans, Black Keys T-shirt, and flip-flops, rummaging through the fridge, Alice was tempted to tell her she was no longer allowed access to food. She

wanted to lock Denise in her room for the rest of high school
and feed her through a slit. She couldn't believe that her daughter
was behaving exactly like she had in high school. After all, she
had reasons to rebel—her parents were traveling all the time, her
sister was dead. What had Denise ever had to contend with?
Alice had devoted her entire life to her children, and now it was
clear that her sacrifices had made no difference at all.

Denise seemed content sitting in her room playing her guitar and
roaming around town with her friends on the weekends. She would
never get into a competitive college with her grades; admission was
far more competitive these days. Ed was at least partially to blame; he
didn't care if she smoked pot since he'd smoked plenty of it himself.
If Denise got a C on her report card, Alice was outraged, but Ed just
commiserated with her, going so far as to say he'd never been much
of a student either. He had the habit of telling people what they
wanted to hear. It was one of his greatest flaws, though Alice had to
admit that it was mild in comparison to her own parents, who had
no problem letting everyone around them down.

There were only sixty-seven students left at the Mt. Carmel School
for the Blind. The school ran year-round with a month long break
in August. But this August, after graduation—after thirty-six years
teaching—Mary Whelan would move to Traverse City to live with
her sister Anna, and there was a possibility that the school, which
had stood on the northwest corner of New Hope Road for a century, might close for good. No dearth of blind students had forced
the possible shutdown—it was just due to the working eyes of

their parents, the ones who had to drive through the east side and down New Hope Road every day bearing witness to the prairie grass, the abandoned buildings, the burnt-out cars, and the young men with firearms who roamed the nightmarish streets.

If the shutdown took place, planting the garden would prove a futile exercise, but Mary Whelan's husband Brendan had died two years before of pancreatic cancer, and with him had gone her retirement dreams. She had no children of her own, and though she'd never mistaken her students for her children, she'd wanted to leave them with one parting gift. She'd always wanted to plant a garden in the side yard; since Brendan's death, it was the only desire for which she could summon any enthusiasm at all.

The students had been thrilled, especially eleven-year-old Gina Sutton, who lived in a tiny walk-up three blocks from the school.

Gina was the first person to whom Mary had mentioned the garden. They were in the rec room sitting at a table playing Crazy Eights. Mary had said, "I want to plant a garden," then stopped abruptly. No matter how she framed it, planting a garden in a school where no one could see it was bound to sound ludicrous.

"I love flowers," Gina said immediately. "I remember seeing them. Honeysuckle. Sometimes we can smell honeysuckle at my house. It grows in the field out back of our building. On the way to school there's wild lavender and mint." Gina lived with her grandmother Lara, who was housebound due to severe osteoarthritis that had bent her back into a down-turned cup. They relied on the generosity of the Mt. Elliot Baptist Church's meals-on-wheels program for their dinners, and Gina ate her only other meal at lunch during school. They owned a refrigerator but it hadn't worked for years. Prenatal drug use had contributed to Gina's ocular atrophy and numerous learning disabilities as well as various vitamin deficiencies more often associated with the developing world.

She'd lost her sight at the age of six, but she knew about the flowers lining the sidewalk because, on occasion, when her neighbor Daniel Lee was agitated and unable to sleep, or working the early shift at the car wash, he walked her to school. He lived a floor below and was sixteen. A tiny boy for his age—just five foot three and slight of frame—he was often in trouble with the law, and he'd spent six months last year in juvenile detention. His mother had died two years before of stomach cancer.

Daniel's grandfather had been a farmer, and when Gina asked him about it, he'd been able to name the flowers—the field clover, golden ragwort, and phlox—that lined the perimeter of the sidewalk. His favorites were the weeds they could pick and eat—purslane, chickweed, dandelions—and she'd trusted him enough to taste each one, though most were bitter. During these promenades, he honed in on the flowers she might touch or smell, but never mentioned the wild strawberry plant next to the Voodoo Lounge or the men who stood silent and slit-eyed next to it, signaling to him about the packets he would distribute later. But she knew.

"What do all of those people want from you?" she'd ask after they passed by.

"How did you know they were there?"

"They're giving off heat."

Over spring break, Mary Whelan traveled to Cleveland, Ohio and visited the Rosemary Gongwer Talking Garden for the Blind. She copied the layout and returned to Mt. Carmel, laying down sheets of paper all over the side yard and then filling those spaces in with flowers she bought herself. She worked slowly; it took her three months. No one on staff offered any assistance, though some of the students showed up on the weekends to lend a hand. The other teachers spent the spring inside the lounge, grousing about the possible shutdown and circling job listings in the education section of the newspaper. They thought Mary was deluded.

The only people who paid her any attention were the monks who lived across the street in the Still Point Zen Buddhist Temple. They monitored her comings and goings—or so it seemed to her—and sometimes when the bags of potting soil made her stagger, one of them would scurry across the street to help. In their tightly wound robes they appeared to be gliding up and down the street on an invisible conveyor belt. She could never tell them apart: black, white, or Asian, shorn heads and glasses. Conversation might have helped her delineate, but beyond offering aid, they said nothing.

In the morning when Mary arrived at school, she often saw them sitting on the long porch that ran the length of their redbrick hovel of a temple. The sight of them cross-legged on their cushions, eyes closed, thumb and index fingers touching, oblivious to the seamy world of New Hope Road, annoyed her. Though the inscription above their front door read, "If a man lives a pure life nothing can destroy him," Mary had seen her share of innocent people hammered like nails. She couldn't understand the monks, but she couldn't fault them either. Without their help, she would never have finished her garden. In the final stages of construction, they had come over to help run the water and the electricity so that the fountain in the center shot geysers at ten-second intervals and the Braille cards talked.

Alice hadn't been to this part of Detroit since she'd once made a drug run for her boyfriend Mike in high school, years before. New Hope Road was the same road where LaDonta the dealer had lived. Driving down it, Alice felt like she'd entered an apocalypse.

"Shit," Denise said. "Where the hell are you taking me, Mom?"

"The blind school."

Denise slunk down in her seat. "You really do want to kill me."

Mt. Carmel School for the Blind had been standing on New Hope Road since Alice was a kid. She remembered seeing it when she was at LaDonta's buying pot. Back then, the school had been in relatively good shape. Now the building appeared to be collapsing in on itself. Across the street, LaDonta's row house was gone as were all the other houses on the block.

The only other building on New Hope Road that appeared inhabited was a dilapidated temple on the corner, with a sign above the door, which read "Still Point Zen Buddhist," and a small ebony Buddha overturned in a birdbath in the yard. There were several Monks sitting in folding chairs on the front porch.

The windows on the first and second floors of the blind school were covered with bars to keep out vandals and thieves. No foliage ornamented the front of it. Alice and Denise hurried up to the imposing oak door and rang the bell. A small-boned woman with springy white hair and neon-colored reading glasses opened it and introduced herself as Mary Whelan. She wore big baggy jeans that pooled around her ankles, and a plain white men's undershirt emphasized her gelatinous middle. She was carrying a small trowel.

"I'll give you a little background before we go out," she said. "Let's go to the rec room."

The rec room was a large, sunny room with peeling white paint and floor-to-ceiling windows. About a dozen wooden card tables were clumped together. On the north end, two paisley couches faced a twenty-inch television, which was tuned to *The Today Show*. Though there were more than two dozen children seated, the room was as quiet as a chapel. Most of the blind children were reading, running their hands over their big Braille books, but a few were playing cards and one or two were stationed in front of the TV, their heads angled toward it.

A couple of kids turned toward Mary as she passed and said, "Hello, Mrs. Whelan." They were walking on thick carpeting, making no discernable noise, and yet it seemed like everyone had detected their arrival.

When they left the room, Alice asked how the blind kids knew they were passing through.

"They notice everything," Mary said. "My perfume. The way I walk. Apparently one leg hits the floor harder than the other."

She led Denise and Alice outside to the garden. In the middle stood a large fountain, a five-level rock-pond waterfall with geysers. An aural focal point, Mary had placed it first— before the planting—in the middle of the wheel. The garden branched out from the five-tiered fountain into five spokes. One led to the fragrant garden where the lavender, thyme, verbena, and sage offered a symphony of smells. One to the vegetables, where the students would be encouraged to touch and even taste the tomatoes, garlic, and peppers. The others to the tactiles, the herbs, and the butterfly garden. A second fountain was donated by the monks, who had dropped it off one Saturday morning while Mary was planting carrots. It was a wall fountain of the Buddha, water pouring out through his hands. They mounted it at the end of the third spoke amid the bed that would accommodate the hyacinths, lilies, and gardenias. The smallest fountain was a fishpond donated the week before by Sheila Naster, the principal, who, Mary felt, had probably done it out of guilt. One day soon, it would be flanked on either side by shoulder-high sunflowers. Mary had put several goldfish in the pond. Each garden plot was bricked in and raised two feet above the path so that the students would not have to stoop to access the floral bouquet and those in wheelchairs could reach out and run their fingers over the blossoms.

"I need some help with the touch and butterfly plants," Mary said. "That's all we have left to do before the big opening. The children also planted sunflowers in pots and we have to replant those on the right. The opening is June fifteenth, so we only have a little over a week to finish." She turned to Denise. "How long will you be with us?"

"The *whole* week," Denise said, not trying to hide the fact that she was disgusted.

"Great," Mary said. "I'll just walk your mother out."

Mary led Alice to the wrought iron gate and told her to return at three thirty.

"You can go out here and walk around to the front of the school. In the future, why don't you park right outside the garden and I'll be waiting for you. I'm always out here by eight."

The six-foot wrought iron gate was fashioned into two conjoined hearts. Mary unlocked it and let Alice out. When she closed the gate, Alice noticed that the outside of the redbrick facade was covered with graffiti. She'd been cast back into hell.

Steve Hoben sat on the porch in full lotus watching the elegant woman in the black pantsuit hurrying back to her Mercedes, the same car his ex-wife probably drove now that she was married to Van Marrick, the real estate mogul. He'd seen the woman arrive with a girl, who couldn't have been a potential student as he kept pushing her bangs aside to see. She was about the same age as Steve's own daughter who lived in Colorado and whom he hadn't seen in close to a year.

Steve should not have noticed her at all. He was supposed to be meditating. But for the past several months he'd been unable to close his eyes on New Hope Road even for a second. He'd spent four years at the monastery striving for peace of mind, only to have an intruder hit him over the head with a brick and shatter his illusions of detachment. He'd spent a month in the hospital and still suffered excruciating headaches and what he called "wobbly mind."

The woman sat in the car with her hands on the wheel. Around him, the other monks sat with their eyes closed or lowered three feet in front of them, led by Master Hui-Chao, who'd transcended the mugging immediately.

The boys who'd attacked them could have been easily identified—the one who'd knocked Steve down had a bright-blue butterfly tattooed on his upper right arm—but Master Hui-Chao refused to do it. Instead he had the nerve to quote the Dhammapada:

> Not by enmity are enmities quelled,
>
> Whatever the occasion here.
>
> By the absence of enmity are they quelled.
>
> This is an ancient truth.

The woman across the street leaned forward and rested her head on her steering wheel. Was she crying? Her shoulders were shaking. Steve got up and walked down the front steps. He crossed the street slowly, knowing that if he rapped on her window he would startle her. She looked over when he was a few feet away and swiped at her eyes, embarrassed. The window came down.

"I'm sorry," she said. "I'm fine. You probably thought there was something wrong."

"I just wanted to check. I didn't know if you needed help." The woman looked like a celebrity with her perfectly coifed hair and painted nails. Her skin was as smooth as the stone Buddha in the front yard. He felt like he'd seen her somewhere before.

She ran a finger under both eyes to wipe away her mascara, but only managed to smear it more.

"I just dropped my daughter off to help in the garden. She's a teenager . . . you know that age . . ."

Steve told her about his three children.

"Oh, you can marry?"

"Some of us . . ." He didn't add, "And divorce, and lose their children in a horrific custody battle."

"Just like Protestant ministers, I suppose." She smiled and pointed toward the temple. "And you've been here for a long time?"

"The monastery has been here for decades. I've been here four years."

"You have much of a . . . congregation here?"

"Not really." Immediately this question brought the intruders to mind, those who had definitely not entered the monastery in search of enlightenment.

"I know this sounds bad, but I don't know how you can stand it." She nodded toward the run-down neighborhood. "I didn't think it was possible, but this area is even worse than when I was growing up."

"The fruit of evil deeds is being gathered now," Steve said, quoting Master Hui-Chao like he normally did without thinking, but this time the minute he said it a great wave of fury overtook him.

Before the woman could respond, he said, "We are taught not to complain. The sutra tells us not to worry about the ills around us because when things are surveyed by a higher intelligence, the foundation of causation is reached."

"Hmm . . . I'll have to share that theory with my husband."

"But the truth is, it's hard for anyone to transcend this," Steve said, turning back to look at the monastery and the porch where Master Hui-Chao had opened his eyes.

Mary had put Denise in the touch plants; she showed her the silky lamb's ears, sharp agave, cinnamon fern, curly mint, heartleaf bergenia, horehound, and tunic flower.

Denise was dying to lie down in the dirt, but she kept planting because Mary was kneeling in the next bed, keeping a close eye on her.

When her father had found out about Denise's punishment, he had laughed, picturing her in a garden. Then he slapped Denise on the back, gripping her shoulder tightly. "I've been telling your mother this is just a stage," he said. "We both know you've had enough of getting in trouble. I'm sure this will never happen again."

Denise had agreed, but even if she hadn't, her father would have turned back to his paperwork. He never asked Denise any questions even though he queried people in his plant about their lives and often appeared mesmerized by their tales of woe, incensed by any perceived injustices. Her father's employees gushed about their compassionate employer and Denise often fantasized about shouting out the truth, that her father was just putting on a performance to ensure their loyalty, that the minute he walked away he would turn back to his poetry books and forget about their existence altogether.

Denise watched as a small black girl with a white stick emerged from the building, ticking her stick back and forth as she made her way down the path toward the five-tiered fountain. Once there, the girl stopped and ran her fingers under the water, then turned around to face the beds, trying to decide which direction to take—left toward the vegetables or right to the touch plants. How would she choose? Denise sat with the potted lamb's ear in her hand, a red plastic cup full of lemonade wedged into the dirt beside her, waiting for the girl's next move. When the girl started down the path toward her, Denise tried not to make any noise, but the girl stopped right in front of her anyway.

"Who are you?" she asked.

"How did you know I was here?" It had popped out of her mouth, and Denise felt her face heat up.

"The sound."

The girl's eyes oscillated back and forth. Looking at them made Denise dizzy.

"You don't know what you're doing, do you?" the girl said. "You've just been sitting there doing nothing the whole time I been out here. How old are you? What's your name?"

"I'm doing community service. I'm seventeen. My name is Denise." Denise had been gripping the plant so hard it had sprung free of the pot and was shedding dirt. She rotated around into a kneeling position and tried to smash it into the hole she had dug, but the hole was too shallow. She placed it back in the pot, reached for her small shovel, and started digging. "I had to come," she added. "I got in some trouble."

"For what?"

"Drugs."

"Are you going to jail?" The girl leaned forward, searching for ground. When she found the raised bed, she ran her fingers through the dirt, massaging it before sitting down on the spot she'd cleared.

Denise laughed. "Not yet."

"You go to jail for drugs. That's what happened to Daniel."

"Who's Daniel?" Denise started on another hole.

"My neighbor. He walks me to school sometimes when he's working at the car wash. His mother died and he started dealing. Got six months. He told me he won't do it again but I bet they'll make him. Why do you sell drugs when you're rich?"

"I don't sell drugs." Denise had moved away from the girl to pick up another plant and she stopped, pot in midair. "How do you know I'm rich?"

"They gave you a second chance."

Denise was silent the entire way home, her head turned toward the window. That night at dinner she said, "I spent the day in this wicked part of town."

She was addressing Alice, but the way she said it—loudly, with emphasis and a rising note at the end—indicated that she wanted her father's attention. Oblivious, Ed kept reaching for the potatoes and even snapped his fingers when Alice failed to hand them to him quickly enough.

"Wicked, meaning?" Alice asked as Ed heaped mashed potatoes onto his plate.

"Wicked meaning wicked."

"Oh," Alice said. "I thought wicked was slang for 'cool.'"

Elise, the Polish housekeeper, tapped lightly and slipped through the swinging door from the kitchen, bearing food.

The phone rang and Elise went back into the kitchen to get it. It was for Ed, of course.

"Of all the . . ." Ed clapped the table with his free hand. "I have to take this. It's probably Richard. I'll get it upstairs."

Richard Hendel was a plant manager, the one who let Ed in on all the nitty-gritty. Denise and Alice watched Ed hurry up the stairs to his third-floor office with his plate in hand. He wouldn't be back down anytime soon. Alice glanced over at Denise, who was staring down at her plate, her elbow on the table, her cheek resting on her left hand.

"So, you were saying . . . about the garden?" Alice lifted a forkful of mashed potatoes to her mouth.

"That was it," Denise said, with a shrug. "It was wicked."

For the rest of the week Alice drove Denise to the school, waving at Steve, who always noticed her returning to her car and never seemed to be meditating with the same fervor as the other monks.

Every day when Denise returned home from the garden, she went right up to her room and didn't surface until seven or eight, when she emerged for dinner. On Friday afternoon, Alice asked her if she was glad that the gardening stint was over. Alice was happy she wouldn't have to navigate through Detroit anymore and she was about to say so when Denise announced that she'd like to return the following Saturday for the grand opening of the garden. A little girl named Gina had asked her to take some pictures of the garden for her grandmother, who was housebound and wouldn't be able to attend.

Alice was shocked, but she knew better than to show it. The last thing she wanted was to drive back to the ghetto, but maybe Denise was going to turn her life around, and if so, it would be wrong to discourage it.

On Saturday, Alice insisted that Ed accompany them to the grand opening as a show of solidarity, but she regretted it the minute he pulled out his iPhone and started tapping away. The whole ride down he never looked up once.

Mary Whelan arrived at the school just before seven. Anticipating a crowd—there had been a nice article in the life section of the *Free Press*—Mary had pulled up to the rear of the building with five-dozen doughnuts. She'd bought them at Marge's Donut Shop that morning, thinking the garden had cost her a huge chunk of her meager retirement savings. But who cared, really? The children would always remember the effort she'd made.

She placed the doughnuts down on the counter and went into the pantry to retrieve the coffee. Someone had forgotten to take out the trash and a rodent had overturned the can. She picked up the mess and headed out the front door toward the dumpster located just beyond the garden gate.

The monks were supposed to wake up at four forty-five every morning. The first sitting meditation commenced at five, followed by a second one at nine. If the weather was agreeable, Master Hui-Chao liked them to convene on the porch. Since there were only seven of them living at the monastery, there was plenty of room to place the cushions along the long wooden expanse. The morning the garden was set to open, Steve overslept, missing the five o'clock meditation for the first time in four years. When he went out on the porch at seven he was surprised to find Master Hui-Chao still there.

Steve had not tried to hide the fact that the attack had altered him. He'd consulted Master Hui-Chao on many occasions, but all of his advice—open to the world around him, invite the demons in, compassion for all sentient beings—did not resonate with him. Why should their attackers get away with it? Why should he let it go?

This morning Master Hui-Chao was sitting at the far end of the porch in one of the plastic folding chairs the monks put out for visitors. Most of the time he appeared so ethereal, but sitting there with his arms crossed tightly over his chest he resembled what he had once been, a middle-aged banker, staring across the street at the wrought iron entrance to the garden.

Steve took the seat next to him. Master Hui-Chao reached for his hand. There were tears in his eyes when he turned to face Steve.

"This may be hard for you," he said.

Steve turns toward the street, but he can't make sense of what he's seeing. There's a rose bush jammed into a sewer in the middle of the street like a centerpiece, flowers scattered all over the pavement. Across the street, Mary Whelan makes a sound like a small animal with its leg caught in a trap. The garbage bag slips out of her hand and the contents spill; an industrial-sized can of Hunt's tomato sauce rolls into the street.

While Steve and Master Hui-Chao are running toward her, she falls, slowly, like the woman in the opera who has stabbed herself with a knife and has to sing an aria before she dies. Master Hui-Chao is at her side by the time she hits the ground, but halfway across the street Steve slips on a large clump of blue flowers. He gets there after the fact.

Master Hui-Chao scoops Mary up by one arm and Steve grabs the other. They help her over to the one bench still intact.

The other three benches—donations from alumni—have been hatcheted to pieces. The five-tiered fountain lies on its side, the hose detached, the flowers hacked off their stalks. The tulips hang over the fishpond like victims of a firing squad. The left side of the gate has been kicked in. The Buddha's head is cracked in half, jammed upside down into the gate's conjoined heart so that the smile is inverted.

"Did you see who did it?" Steve whispers to Master Hui-Chao after they've placed Mary on the bench.

"Yes."

He's so calm Steve has the urge to punch him. "And you didn't call anyone? You didn't yell?"

"It would not have stopped them."

Master Hui-Chao wipes off the bench next to Mary and sits down beside her. Mary doesn't turn or respond to the conversation. She stares straight at the fountain without moving, her mouth slightly ajar.

"Yes, it would have! You could have stopped them!" Steve's hands tighten into fists. "How many times are you going to let things just happen?"

Steve turns and walks away so quickly that he has to lift his robes to keep them from bunching up around his calves. He flees down the street, away from the garden and the monastery. Three blocks later, he rests on the curb across from a lone redbrick apartment building, burying his head in his bent knees. What kind of a fool watches and does nothing? How could anyone be so misguided? He has to leave the monastery today, find a new path, one that doesn't call for bearing witness to all this crap.

"You OK?"

It's one of the blind students. She's standing on the sidewalk above Steve with a young man, just a little taller, who can obviously see and is now scowling.

Steve doesn't know how long they've been there. He swipes at his face to clear the tears. He stands up, ignoring the boy's angry face.

"I'm OK," he says.

"This is Daniel," the girl says. "I'm Gina."

"I was just taking a walk. I live in the monastery across the street from your school. I'm a monk."

"What kind of monk?" Daniel mumbles.

The kind who cries and can't stop, Steve thinks. "A Buddhist monk," he says, and dusts off his robes.

"That don't mean nothing to me," Daniel says.

"Me neither," Steve mutters.

"Are you coming to the opening?" Gina gazes in Steve's direction, her large eyes roaming.

Steve says nothing. He can't bring himself to tell her. He and Daniel eye each other. Finally, Daniel shrugs and takes Gina's arm. They start off toward the school. Steve follows, bringing up the rear, his feet so numb it's an effort to lift them. He knows he should call out to warn them, but he can't. When they reach the corner of New Hope Road, Daniel stops and leans over to pick up a lone yellow rose lying upturned on the ground. His sleeve slides up and Steve catches sight of the vivid blue on his upper arm, the butterfly tattoo.

"Rose." Gina smiles and presses it to her face.

"You!" Steve lunges, grabbing for the tattooed arm.

When he latches on, Daniel lets out a high-pitched shriek.

"Daniel! What's going on?" Gina's fingers rise up in front of her body, her anxious digits like ten tiny people locked in a dark room fumbling for a door. "Leave Daniel alone. You leave him alone!"

Gina's distressed face stops Steve. His clenched fist drops to his side. "You little shit! You nearly killed me. Now you destroyed the garden. You . . ."

Daniel shakes his head vehemently, his forehead glistening at the perimeter of his tight curls. "I didn't do it, they did."

"They?" Steve shouted. "They? You mean you and your . . . posse?"

"Nah, not me."

"Do you have any idea what you did to me?" Steve's face is hot, his breath shallow.

"I didn't touch you, man."

"You ruined it."

"The garden?" Gina's cornrows swing back and forth across her face. "There's nothing wrong with the garden."

"Shit," Daniel says. "I wouldn't fuck with Gina's garden."

"I meant me," Steve says, and pounds on his own chest.

"I'm telling you, man, I didn't do nothing."

"Nothing is wrong with the garden," Gina says with conviction.

Steve wants to tell the boy to fuck off, but he's having trouble catching his breath.

Gina yanks on Daniel's arm. "Let's go. Don't just stand there. I'm going to miss it."

Daniel glares at Steve. It's impossible to tell what his glare means. Maybe it means that he doesn't care what Steve thinks, that Steve deserved the beating. Maybe it means he doesn't even remember it.

"You have the tattoo," Steve says, and points a shaky finger. "You did it."

"This?" Daniel holds his arm up.

"Is he talking about the butterfly?" Gina's fingers run up and down Daniel's arm. "The one you all got for your mama?"

Steve turns away from them and leans over, thinking he's going to puke. When he straightens up, Gina and Daniel are gone.

On New Hope Road the crowd of parents and journalists and neighborhood residents is three deep, clamoring over each other to peer into the garden. Steve reaches the corner just as Daniel leads Gina into the thick of it. The crowd unzips and then coalesces again around them. A moment later Daniel returns to the street without her. Two boys wearing what look like black ski caps motion to him, and he scrambles up a tree across the street where, Steve supposes, they will be able to enjoy the havoc on the street below.

A silver Mercedes pulls up and parks underneath where the three boys are perched in the tree. *Bad idea*, Steve thinks. The woman Steve has been watching all week emerges with her daughter. It's hard for them to negotiate the crowd, but eventually they push through. A man in a pin-striped suit follows them out of the car calling, "Alice!" but either she doesn't hear him or she doesn't care.

Steve keeps walking and scowls at the tree as he passes it. The boys don't even notice. The throng parts for him for no apparent reason, without any indication that he actually wants to progress. When he reaches the gate, he sees the blind students lined up at the side door, the principal holding them back. He's about to turn back toward the monastery when a hand clamps down on his shoulder.

"Will you take him in? I have to go to work," says a large man with a buzz cut in a workman's jumpsuit. The name tag on the jumpsuit says, "Rick." The man is pointing to a young blind boy of about ten with a shock of carrot-red hair. The boy fastens onto Steve before he can protest.

Gina is leading the procession from the side door into the garden when Steve and the red-haired boy join the lineup. She is being guided by the rich woman's daughter. They head toward the fragrant garden. *What in the world are they doing? What is there to see?* Steve glances over to the bench where Mary Whelan is still sitting, rocking back and forth rhythmically, watching the children through half-closed eyes, her face as white as the vermiculite the monks helped her mix into the soil the week before.

Steve follows the group down the path, watching his feet until the feet in front of him come to a halt. Glancing up to get his bearings, he notices that the procession has stopped in front of the fragrant garden.

Master Hui-Chao is sitting lotus in the raised bed amid a scattering of broken, trampled flowers. In one hand, he holds a bunch of smashed lavender, in the other one mint leaf. Beyond him, a monk sits in the touch garden, another in the vegetables. Five altogether in the garden, one in each spoke of the wheel.

As Gina approaches, Master Hui-Chao lifts the flowers so that they extend out over the walkway directly in front of her face. She leans in to smell them. Mary Whelan moans. A woman standing behind her reaches down and touches her shoulder. Farther back, something clatters to the ground near the rich woman and she bends down to retrieve it.

Gina breathes in the fragrance, her eyes closed. Without moving she says, "Denise? Can you take the picture now?"

The rich woman's daughter is holding a fancy black camera. *Spoiled brat*, Steve thinks. He looks over at the girl's parents again. The woman is straightening up, holding an iPhone in her hand. She nudges her husband, who obviously dropped it, but he's busy watching his daughter, so she slips it back into his shirt pocket.

Master Hui-Chao looks like he is levitating on a flower carpet. The girl snaps several more close-ups. When she's done, she bends down to smell the flowers as well.

"Beautiful," Gina calls out as she moves toward the next station. "Thank you, Mrs. Whelan."

Master Hui-Chao lifts the flowers to let the procession pass by. Gina walks slowly toward the next garden plot, her classmates forming a long beaded strand behind her. As Steve passes, Master Hui-Chao nods at him and points toward the gate. Steve follows his gaze out to the elm tree across the street, where Daniel and two other boys are sitting on the low-hanging limbs, watching their progress down the path.

acknowledgments

"Use Everything in Your Arsenal," *Kenyon Review* (KRO) Summer, 2011

"A Shift in the Weather," *Florida Review,* 2015

"Trees from Heaven," *Dogwood Journal,* 2007

"The Guest Room," *Windsor Review,* 2008

"Opportunity Cost," *Montreal Review,* 2012

"Garden for the Blind," honorable mention, 2012 *Tiferet* fiction contest